Northern Edge

Northern Edge

A NOVEL BY

Barbara Quick

HarperCollins *West*

A Division of HarperCollins*Publishers*

A hardcover edition of this book was published by Donald I. Fine, Inc., and in Canada by General Publishing Company Limited.

First HarperCollins West edition published in 1995.

Library of Congress Cataloging-in-Publication Data
Quick, Barbara.
    Northern edge : a novel of survival in Alaska's Arctic / Barbara Quick.—1st HarperCollins West ed.
        p.   cm.
    ISBN 0–06–258521–5
    1. Wilderness survival—Arctic regions—Fiction.   2. Wilderness survival—Alaska—Fiction.   3. Women—Arctic regions—Fiction.
    4. Women—Alaska—Fiction.   I. Title.
    [PS3567.U285N6   1995]
    813'.54—dc20   94-30326
                                                                                            CIP

95 96 97 98 99 (RRDCH) 10 9 8 7 6 5 4 3 2 1

This edition is printed on acid-free paper that meets the American National Standards Institute Z39.48 Standard.

For János

One

Catherine and I are sitting on our second favorite bench at lunch-hour, eating pasta salad. The students are back; the place is crawling with them. "You've got to leave," says Catherine, who has worked here for eighteen years.

"I don't know what else I'd do." I haven't been feeling well lately, but the doctor says there's nothing wrong with me. I worry about things. About cancer. About feeling too depressed to get out of bed in the morning. About poor people, especially mothers who can't give their children enough to eat.

"Drive a truck," says Catherine. "Teach English in Japan."

"It's too easy to stay."

"Tell me about it," says Catherine.

I look down at my feet. I'm wearing black pumps. I'm wearing a dress with shoulder pads. The professors treat us like some species of subhuman. "I've been waiting for something to happen," I say.

"Nothing *happens*," says Catherine. "The days just run into each other. What did you do last Thursday?"

I think about it a moment. "I can't remember."

"There," says Catherine.

"There what?"

"There, I told you so. Your life has turned into a big blur. A lava flow. All that's happening is that you're getting older."

"I hate you, Catherine," I say, looking down at my feet again.

"You *should* hate me. I'm what you'll become if you stay here."

I look at Catherine, who is striking a pose in all her wretched administrative-assistantness. Her suit is perfect. Her blouse is silk. She has two little black hairs sprouting on her chin.

"I'm not thirty yet," I say.

"You'll be thirty next year."

I've already told Catherine I hate her (I love her, really). I have nothing left to say.

The Dean drops a report on my desk on his way back into his office after lunch. He stops and looks at me with a puzzled expression, as if for a moment he has forgotten who I am. Then he smiles. "Tay," he says. He is about sixty, but he still has acne.

"Dean Cooter," I say.

"Next Tuesday, dear. I need it for the regents meeting. Think you can manage?"

I leaf through the report. About half of it is handwritten, but after four years I'm better at reading his handwriting than he is. There are several complicated charts that are much too wide for the page. I imagine for a moment his reaction if I were to call *him* "dear." Catherine and I call him "the Cootie."

"If the Xerox machine doesn't break down. If Amos Merrick doesn't have another crisis with his course notes."

The Cootie waves his hand in the air: these are clearly not possibilities. "Splendid, then," he says. "Next Tuesday. Early morning, please: I have to catch a plane. Come to think of it, Monday night would be even better."

I smile my best executive secretary smile.

"That's my girl," says Dean Cooter. He walks into his office and shuts the door for his afternoon snooze.

It's the fourth day of the semester and I've met most of the new graduate students. There is a preponderance of foreigners with bad skin, young men who look as though they've been eating nothing but Big Macs and french fries since arriving in this country. Morgie stops by my desk.

"New ensemble?" I ask him.

He touches the thin, nubby tie that contrasts stylishly with his raw-silk shirt. "Picked it up in Georgetown."

"Oh, Morgie," I say. I've missed him, but I'm afraid he's tired of hearing me say so. It makes him feel guilty, he says. We're still friends, but now Morgie lives with a young history student instead of me: a beautiful slim boy from Chico. Morgie suddenly decided he was gay last year—as if one decides these things.

"How's Jonathan?" I ask.

"Oh, you know. He's in a big snit because I didn't take him to Washington."

I nod, prepared to let Morgie walk past me into the Cootie's office (Dean Cooter is Morgie's thesis advisor). He touches my arm. "Feeling any better?"

This is a mistake: I'm not wearing waterproof mascara. I can feel the heat rising in my neck and face. "Go away," I tell Morgie.

"I'm sorry," he says for the two hundredth time.

"It doesn't matter," I tell him. The worst of it is that I had hoped he'd get his doctorate and we'd get married and have a baby. I can picture Morgie pinning a diaper with great engineering precision.

I have decided to bleach the hair on my upper lip (on a man, it's called a mustache). Buying the little kit in the drugstore is a humiliating experience: I imagine that the cashier—a young girl in her late teens who is still worrying about pimples—is peering at my face just below my nose. At least when a boy buys his first condom, he is headed on the path of his own quite normal sexuality. But why do women have mustache hair? It's not very dark and it's not coarse, but it's there; and it wasn't there before. Is it because I haven't had children? Is that why Catherine has those hairs—do the gods say, "Well, there's no sense in having her be a woman, anyway: let's give her a mustache!"?

In my bathroom, with the door locked (even though I'm here by myself), I mix a quarter teaspoon of the "accelerator" powder with a half teaspoon of the cream. I smash them together on the white plastic palette provided and then smear the paste in two thick white dabs above my lip. I sit on the toilet seat leafing through The Bay Guardian until fifteen minutes have elapsed by my wristwatch. Then I scrape the stuff off and wash it down the sink. I wash my face and then pat it dry.

In the mirror, the hair is perfectly blond but my skin is red from the bleach. I put the box away in the medicine cabinet with the product name facing inward so that no stray browser will notice that I possess such a thing: so that no man will ever think about my mustache.

I am on a date with a visiting post-doc from England. We're eating at a Cuban restaurant. We're on the salad course. I have always been a pushover for accents. When I close my eyes and just listen, I can almost imagine falling in love with him. When I open them I see a man who looks like a slightly plump version of Mick Jagger. He has the sad, rotten teeth of the working class.

"Did you like Alaska?" I ask him. He has just returned from spending a summer there on an oil rig.

"Fabulous," he says. It comes naturally to him to talk like that. I imagine what it would be like to hear him call me "Dahling!" I sigh and he puts his hand over mine on the table. I feel absolutely nothing: it's as if he has put a slab of clay over my hand. I wonder if I'm becoming frigid.

"I've thought of applying for a job up there sometime."

"For the money?" he asks me.

I smile, determined to be honest for a change. "For the men," I tell him.

"Well, then," he says, removing his hand. "I've heard it's a five-to-one ratio."

"Did a light go on in my eyes?" I ask him.

"They're lovely eyes," he says. "Gray-green—always been my favorite. Have you ever thought of growing your hair long?"

I reach for my glass of ice-water. Type three: controlling bully. Pygmalion syndrome. Fancies he's found a diamond in the rough. "It's too fine," I tell him. "It just looks straggly. I've got to wash it every day for it to even look *this* good."

"It's nice hair. I was just picturing how it would look long."

I'm picturing his pictures: Lizzie Siddel with her head thrown back, her straw-colored masses of hair waving like the ocean. I smile, feeling sorry for him. "What century would you live in if you could choose?"

He looks at me with some surprise. "The nineteenth. Darwin's century—I've always thought so." I smile, feeling satisfied with myself. Then suddenly I feel unutterably lonely.

"Do you know of anyplace I could apply for a job there?"

He looks puzzled. "In the nineteenth century?"

"In Alaska."

"Oh, of course. Hum. James and Jacobs might have something. They're always looking for good office people." He takes a card out of his wallet: an environmental consulting firm, Fairbanks. "You might send them your résumé." I slip the card into my pocket (it would just get lost in my satchel).

I am walking across campus: it's eight-fifteen. I'm allowed to come in at eight-thirty because Dean Cooter doesn't get there until nine. This is a source of some resentment among the other secretaries in the department. I also have a key to the third-floor restroom, which has a toaster-oven, a refrigerator, and a couch. This is reserved for the handful of women engineering faculty (this year, there are two), and for higher-level support staff. My shoulders ache and I wonder if it is because I am support staff and the weight has just become too much for me; or whether it's time to clean out my satchel again.

I refer to it, with some embarrassment, as my portable filing cabinet. It has everything in it that a purse usually contains: wallet, checkbook, keys, comb, makeup kit, nail-clipper; plus address book, calculator, about five pens and pencils, note-cards, a to-do list, and usually a magazine or two and a paperback novel or book of short stories. I put bills in there so that I'll remember to pay them during the day. Sometimes they get lost for weeks.

The satchel keeps getting heavier until finally I can't stand it anymore. But I have trouble figuring out which of these things I can do without: suddenly they all seem necessary to my survival.

I walk by the statue in the faculty glade: the art nouveau bronze nymph. I feel a sense of identification with her body—especially the breasts. I feel glad every time I pass here that she lives surrounded by azalea bushes. There are robins all over the damp sloping lawn: scores of them. Steam is rising from the ground. What if I just didn't go to work? I think suddenly; but I keep walking. My high heels click on the asphalt. How many pairs of shoes have I worn out already? Perhaps I will make a sculpture someday out of worn-out high-heeled pumps (Dali did it with es-padrilles, after all).

I stop and sit down on a bench beneath the Campanile: I'll go to work, but perhaps just this once I'll be a little late. I need to think for a moment. I'm wondering if I'll ever make anything. All the work I do disappears: all the hundreds, thousands of sheets of paper that I've typed and mailed and filed. My words disappear after I've spoken them into Dean Cooter's telephone. The outfits that I put together so artfully every year: the silk blouses get worn out and stained; the various skirts and blouses and sweaters and stockings and belts and boots will be cast asunder in Goodwill bins, bought as separate pieces, their artfulness lost forever. All the food I've so carefully prepared for dinner parties at Peg and Denny's: oh, everyone applauded at the time; everyone said how blood will out, and how beautiful!, and her father's daughter; but nothing's left behind of all that. It's all temporary: I've never done anything permanent in my life. Even my love left Morgie completely unchanged (at least he gave me something each time, and, secretly, because I loved him, I liked the seeping wetness afterwards during the day, that bit of him leaking out of me). Oh, Morgie will have his thesis; and then he'll have bridges and buildings and roads.

I keep meaning to apply to graduate school again: I had always thought I'd get a Ph.D. in art history; that, if I couldn't make things myself—lasting things—at least I could write books about the things that other people made.

My parents didn't express an opinion. They are both so busy with their own work—Denny with his paintings, Peg with her children's books. And, anyway, they always made it a policy not to judge me. After I'd finished my undergraduate work at Berkeley, when I didn't get the fellowship at Harvard, they encouraged me to travel. Oh, I traveled beautifully, for almost a year. I could almost taste the colors in Southern France, in Northern Italy; in Holland, in Spain. I guess it's too much to expect that the daughter of a famous painter could possibly have any talent in her hands. And yet I can *see* things, and feel them: there's just no way for the feelings to come out.

My hands are well-coordinated and sturdy-looking. I'm good at fixing things; I have a green thumb. But put a paintbrush in my hands, a palette of colors: my hands go numb.

They won't listen to a word I have to say, the most violent wrenchings of my heart. Sometimes I'd like to eat the colors I see, inside my head and in the world; and I love to touch things. But I'll never make anything out of shapes and colors. They say that sort of talent skips a generation.

I stayed at Peg and Denny's when I got back from Europe and helped them entertain their friends—I even went out with one of the younger ones from time to time, an art printer in his late forties. We were both lonely and afraid. Peg and Denny never said a word, always smiling encouragement and love. It was finally too embarrassing to still be living with my parents, hearing the question when I walked out of a room: And what's Tay *doing* with herself these days? Such a bright pretty girl. The comment was always followed by a sigh; Peg would chirp something cheerful, then change the subject.

I felt that I'd made a failure out of my life. That I'd taken good, promising material and done nothing with it. No artwork. No Ph.D. Not even a husband and kids. I imagined my parents shaking their heads every time I left them alone together. Everything they made turned to gold. Everything but me.

That went on for about six months. Then I went down to the personnel office at the Berkeley campus and filled out the forms for the University's temporary assistance pool. I wowed them on the typing test.

When the first job came through, I found an apartment. Peg and Denny brought me a beautiful house-warming present: a pale pink pottery bowl from Provence, very old and only slightly chipped. On the card, Denny had written in his beautiful calligraphy, *For our daughter, one rare treasure for another*. The bowl sits in a place of honor on my table. Nothing that I could put inside would ever be beautiful enough—or even simple enough. But it was a bowl meant to hold things: fruit or water or rising dough.

I wonder if I'll ever find a man as romantic as Denny. He's old now, but I can remember when he was young and handsome. Peg tells me that he wasn't always so perfect: he drank too much when he was younger, and was often depressed. He lived in Paris in the twenties: what could be more perfect than living in Paris in the twenties and drinking too much and being depressed? Now he does yoga and eats health food. He and Peg walk up Mount Tam every day except when it's raining. My friends ask me, What's it like to have such wonderful parents? Even Morgie's still friends with them.

At nine-forty-five I get to my desk, ready for a good cry. The new work-study receptionist looks at her watch and then smirks at me. Dean Cooter is at a faculty meeting and I don't give a damn what the work-study receptionist thinks. I take out the file that has my name on it, under *M:* Tay MacElroy. My résumé is four years old. I put the Cootie's report off to one side. I start typing a letter to the office manager, James and Jacobs, Fairbanks, Alaska.

I go into Catherine's office and shut the door. She looks up at me, ready for anything. "Are you pregnant?"

I slouch down in a swivel chair, rolling backwards, sticking my legs out. "I've found another job."

Catherine smiles. "Good work." Then sighs. "I'll miss you."

"It's only temporary," I tell her.

"So was this one."

Catherine has a point. "It's in Alaska." I scoot my chair forward and drop the James and Jacobs card on her desk.

We both stare at it. "The office manager is going to have a baby. I'll be taking her place."

"Isn't it cold up there?"

"Two thousand dollars a month, Catherine. And the use of a company car. *And* an apartment."

"It's unbelievable. What's the catch?"

I've considered this myself, but haven't found the answer. "It *is* cold—I looked in my atlas. Forty degrees below zero in the wintertime."

"Will they throw in a lumberjack, too?"

"They didn't say anything about one in writing." Suddenly I can't believe I've done this. I don't know one single person in Fairbanks, Alaska. You probably can't buy a *caffe-latte* there for love or money.

Catherine puts her hand on mine. "*Courage,*" she says in her beautiful French. There wasn't a thing she could do in the Bay Area with that degree of hers: not a thing.

"I'll write to you," I promise her. "And I'm giving two weeks' notice as of today. Do you know anyone who might want to sublet my flat?"

"You'll have it rented in twenty-four hours. Don't tell anyone until you're sure you want to make the commitment."

"Catherine, I'm not sure. That's why I have to fix things so I can't change my mind." I pause to consider. "My nose always turns red when it's cold outside."

"Wear makeup," says Catherine. "I think you're marvelous to do this. It sounds absolutely like an adventure."

I picture myself wearing a wolfskin coat and mushing a team of sled dogs. My composure is perfect, my face an elegant portrait of *sangfroid*—straight out of a Birger Christensen ad in The New Yorker.

Two

~~~~~~~

I'm doing it. I'm on the last leg of the flight, from Seattle to Fairbanks. All night long the sun has been setting. It's still setting when the plane lands. The woman I'm replacing—Pammy Edelman—wrote to say that she'd meet me at the baggage claim. She said she'd be the only six-foot-tall pregnant woman there.

I deplane with that sinking feeling you have when you know that no one will be there for you at the gate, but you look around quickly anyway, without slowing your pace: someone might be there for you. You may have misunderstood the arrangements; you may have forgotten who you are. All around you, other people are hugging, kissing, changing carry-on bags from hand to hand, bestowing loaves of sourdough bread from San Francisco and Mickey Mouse balloons from Disneyland. Not a soul. On my way past the ticket counters toward the baggage claim, I glance to my left and see a monstrously large polar bear rearing up on its hind legs. It's stuffed and behind Plexiglas, but its mouth is open and moist-looking; each toenail has the girth of a sharpened pencil. I make a quick mental search through my memories of National Geographic specials and "Wild Kingdom" segments on TV: no polar bears in Fairbanks—I'm almost sure of it. My two suitcases are just sliding down onto the carousel when a hand slaps down on my shoulder. I glance around to see an overweight, bespectacled man in a jean shirt with dark rings of sweat under his arms.

"MacElroy?"

I look around me, but no one else seems to be responding to the name. I consider pretending that I'm someone else. All I manage is to clear my throat and make a grab for my suitcases as they come around. The man grabs them first. "The truck's out here," he says, striding off toward the double doors. I have to jog to catch up with him.

"I was expecting Pammy Edelman."

"You hungry?" he asks as he throws my bags into the back of a pickup truck that's already half-filled with duffel bags, boxes marked "Flammable," and what look like shotguns in zippered canvas bags. I let myself in on the passenger side.

"No, thank you. They've been feeding us all day and night on the plane." I take the risk of offending him and roll down my window: the man smells like the sort of people in Berkeley who eat out of garbage cans.

He pushes his wire-rimmed glasses further up on his nose. "I apologize if I'm a little ripe, M'am. I just got back from five weeks in the field, and I haven't had a chance to shower yet. Pammy was going to pick you up, but she's having female problems and I was glad to offer my services, seeing as how I had to pick up the rest of my gear at the airport anyway."

"Thanks," I tell him. "I appreciate your taking the trouble."

"You've heard about Pammy?" he asks me.

"She's written me a couple of letters, and I've spoken to her once on the phone." I turn my head to look at Alaska for a moment and breathe some fresh air. "Is she feeling sick or something?"

"Miscarried," says the man. Then he coughs and spits out the window.

"Good Lord," I say. She must have been—I calculate on my fingers—about five months pregnant. I can't even begin to imagine a loss of that magnitude. A five-month-old fetus is halfway there to being a full-grown baby. She must have had to go through labor to deliver it.

"She's okay now. She was in and out of the hospital in a couple of hours. Knowing Pammy, she'll be back at her desk on Monday."

My driver suddenly tears his eyes away from the road and looks across at me. He looks at my arms, my legs, and my feet. He looks at my hands. "You ever done any field work?" he asks me.

I picture Cesar Chavez and his migrant workers in a field of broccoli. "Not much to speak of," I say noncommittally.

He looks heartened. "We've got a crew going out in two days."

I smile in the same way I smile at Dean Cooter.

"It's the Darwin camp, M'am. The comfortablest camp north of the Seward Peninsula."

"Um," I say. "How nice for you. Maybe they'll have showers there."

He's losing patience with me. He continues as if talking to a child. "Pammy's job isn't available anymore, but we've got this position in the field for the next eight weeks."

"I'm an office manager," I tell him. "I type ninety words a minute with no mistakes."

"You ever used binoculars?"

I pause to consider. "At the opera."

The truck careens in a lefthand turn. "I guess that qualifies. Sort of. You know anything about birds?"

"Look, I'm sure this all makes sense to you. But I've been flying all night, I'm very tired, and I'd like to get some sleep."

"I'm taking you to the hotel as fast as I can," he tells me, then mutters something distinctly misogynous under his breath.

The sunset has turned into twilight. Fairbanks is gray— all gray, full of shopping malls and ugly buildings and crisscrossing roads.

My escort breathes deeply, readying himself for another speech. "Pammy told me to tell you the story tonight, so you could think about it before tomorrow."

"Go ahead," I tell him, putting my head back on the seat and closing my eyes.

"We have a seabird study at the Darwin camp on the northwest coast, a couple hundred miles north of Kotzebue. Four of us were going to be going out at first, but Ellen Pearson had to leave town all of a sudden, and all the biologists have made their commitments for the summer. Pammy said that you work out with weights, so Gavin figured that maybe you might not be too sissy to come along as a field assistant." He looks over at me, then starts muttering again. It sounds like, 'Yeah, right. God damn it, Gavin.'

I wonder how ballet classes got translated to working out with weights.

I resent the notion of being thought a sissy. I change the oil on my VW all by myself. I know how to change a tire. Somehow I don't think that either of these things will impress my companion. "I went backpacking for a week-and-a-half once. I can swim three-quarters of a mile."

He says something that sounds like 'Hrrumph.'

"Look, you do have a name, don't you?" I ask him.

"Strider."

"Strider," I repeat. Suddenly I know that if I can just bathe and get a good night's sleep, everything will be all right in the morning. Camp Darwin, indeed! "What sort of work is it, anyway, in—this evolutionary paradise?"

Strider shows his teeth in a smile and I can tell he's been chewing on a plug of tobacco. He has the good, strong, fierce-looking teeth of an animal; his eye teeth are stained a deep yellow. There's tobacco juice in his mustache. "You'll hear all about it tomorrow. Pammy said to tell you that the pay would be, let's see, two hundred dollars a month higher than what she originally offered you for the office job; and all your room, board, field gear, and transportation will be paid for. Pammy was out at Darwin one summer— she liked it."

"Well, I'll think about it, okay?" I step down out of the truck into the parking lot of the Miner's Dream Motor Lodge and Cafe. All I can think about at the moment is a hot shower.

I'm finishing the gold-panner's special breakfast, looking out the window, when Strider's truck drives up. Except Strider doesn't get out of it. I rub my eyes and wish that I had put on makeup.

The man walking toward me is young, tall, bearded, and slim, with a large handsome head and tousled honey-colored hair. He walks right up to me in the coffee shop and sits down across from me in the booth. "You must be Tay," he says. He talks with the way-out-western drawl of a Hollywood cowboy.

I swallow and wipe my mouth with my napkin. "The new girl in town. No one's had any trouble recognizing me so far. How many women *are* there in Fairbanks?"

"Not many as pretty as you, that's for sure. My name is Mike Gavin." He shakes my hand and holds it a little too long. He has dark blue, sparkly eyes.

"I'm really sorry about Pammy," I tell him.

He shakes his head, closing his eyes for a moment. He looks moved. "Pammy's made of tough stuff. She'll get pregnant again."

The waitress comes over and asks if Mike would like to order something. He orders black coffee and I have another cup, covering the thin, chemical taste with packets of cream and sugar.

"So, what's all this about becoming a field-worker?" I wonder if this is the right terminology.

"Well, you were probably in the Seattle airport when Pammy had her miscarriage. It seemed like a shame to fly you all the way up here and then turn you around for home again. And, anyway, you've probably made all sorts of arrangements for being away."

"One or two," I tell him.

"Well, we thought you might like to spend the summer up here anyway, even if you had to work at a different job. I just had a feeling that it might work out. And you're already on the payroll as far as the Houston office is concerned, so it'll be easy as pie to put the new position on the books."

"What *is* the new position?"

"Bio-technician," says Mike Gavin.

It sounds like someone who might run an X-ray machine in a hospital. I think about the prospect of spending eight weeks in a remote field-camp with this man. He's corny but cute. I smile in a way that I hope looks encouraging. "Your friend Strider said something about seabirds."

Mike explains to me that James and Jacobs is in the last stages of completing a ten-year contract to make an environmental assessment of a stretch of coastline somewhere north of the Arctic Circle, prior to offshore leasing. Mike is writing a doctoral dissertation based on the data he's collected about the region's seabird population.

Another doctoral student. I seem to have a talent for them.

"What we do," says Mike, "is go out in little boats and count the birds that nest on the cliffs. We have special plots marked out where we've been looking at the nesting pairs for almost a decade now. We collect some of the birds when they're returning from their feeding grounds and we check out what they've been eating and what sort of shape they're in."

I'm wondering how they get the birds to tell them what they've been eating. I don't want to tell this man that I get seasick. On hot days, I even get carsick. "Do you really think I could help?" I ask him. I'm starting to talk with a western twang myself—it just creeps in.

Mike smiles and pays the bill. We walk outside together, into the parking lot. I shade my eyes and look across the hazy air to a row of trees. "Alaska doesn't look like I expected it to."

"This isn't Alaska. This is a parking lot. They all look alike."

As he starts the motor he says to me, "By the way, you ever used a twelve-gauge shotgun?"

Mike Gavin and I are loaded down with shopping bags filled with clothing from department stores and sporting

goods shops. I have trouble fitting the key into the lock of
my motel room door because I am laughing so hard, and I
can't even remember what got me started. Mike has a way
of just looking at you and getting you going, his eyes full of
mischief. I have new blue jeans, flannel shirts, tee shirts,
turtlenecks, and sweaters. I have an absurd pair of Army-
drab hip boots weighted at the heel and toe with lead: they
reach just below my crotch and hook with two skinny rubber straps over my belt (I have a new leather belt). I have a
Swiss army knife. All of this is compliments of James and
Jacobs. Mike calls it field gear. We have just eaten hamburg-
ers and greasy french fries in the downtown Fairbanks five-
and-dime. I wait until Mike's in the shower before I dig
around in my suitcase for my diaphragm.

We wash ourselves with the miniature bar of Camay
soap provided by the management of the Miner's Dream
Motor Lodge and Cafe. Mike has hair on his back as well as
on his chest. I have never liked the idea of hairy backs before, but on Mike Gavin the phenomenon seems a miracle
of masculine appeal. His body is lean and hard from living
outdoors half the year. We make love in the shower.
Wrapped in towels, we fall on the white chenille bedspread
and before I know it I am looking down at his fine tousled
head between my legs and I am trying not to pull too hard
on his ears. He looks up at me with his dark-blue denim
eyes and when he brings his face close to mine I see the
gleam of all my juices on his mustache and beard.

Afterwards he tucks me into bed between the clean white
sheets. When he turns out the light, it's completely dark:
he's just a voice.

"I'll see you tomorrow morning," he says, kissing me on
the shoulder, then on the mouth. I've already said yes. How
could I not say yes?

After he closes the door, I listen to the sound of toilets flushing and beds creaking and the tide of traffic on the highway. There's a lull in the traffic noise, and I can hear the sound of a drunk outside in the parking lot, crooning or weeping, I can't tell which. Maybe it's a miner who lost his dream. As I fall asleep I remember Catherine's hand on mine. I remember how she said, *Courage!*

Three

~~~~~~~~~~

Alarm clock. Nauseating buzzing (I'm not ready yet, I'm still dreaming—it's warm, deliciously warm). Five-thirty: Mike's coming to pick me up at seven o'clock. I need to pack. I want to look good, too—fresh and clean, fully awake, ready to go to the arctic. In the shower I notice that my thighs are a bit sore, reminiscent of the day after dance class, and I smile all to myself—Mike Gavin. I'm not in love with him—heavens no! It's pure lust. Not even that. Physical happiness: dumb, wordless happiness such as the animals must feel.

Oh, the man and I would have nothing to talk about if we spent more than just a little time together. I'm sure he never reads apart from what he has to read for his doctoral studies—oh, and Playboy Magazine. He probably reads Playboy in the bathroom. But he must have been born with those hands. It's a God-given talent, that instinct for giving pleasure—unlearnable. For a moment, I imagine him in a cozy log cabin watching cartoons on Saturday morning, a half-naked toddler stretched across his lap. He strokes the pale new skin with the flat of his thumb, and the child lies there mesmerized. He probably watches cartoons by himself of a Saturday morning, and has never heard of Henry James, and went to an art gallery once when his cousin from out of town was visiting. I suddenly want to shout at Morgie, You can't base a relationship on physical pleasure alone! I hear myself in the steamy shower mumbling the words, trying them out, even though Morgie is thousands of miles away.

When I'm drying myself off, I take a good long look at my body. Irremediably fair with lots of freckles. Small breasts that look as if they might start drooping before they've ever been used. Fat well in check all over, but the skin is getting tired of holding it all in—no one would mistake these for the buttocks of a young girl. Strawberry blond hair that just reaches my collarbone when dripping wet. It's been ages since I've made love like that—I can't even remember another time. Oh, the perfunctory acrobatics in bed—did you come, now I can come. But not for ages this total loss of self, of self-consciousness: yes, transports of love—I mean, pleasure (must keep them straight—I'm getting as bad as Morgie).

At seven sharp, I'm sitting in the lobby, my carry-on bag neatly packed with my field gear, my large suitcase filled with everything that I'm going to leave behind. I took my diaphragm but packed my watch in the suitcase. (Mike told me to—it's not waterproof, and it's an expensive one: I bought it in Switzerland.)

The blue truck drives up. Strider gets out, nods to me, and pays my hotel bill with a credit card. I climb in next to him. He has just bathed (I can smell the Ivory soap and his aftershave); his gray-streaked hair is slicked back. "Where's Mike?" I ask.

"Oh, he and Phoebe went to the airport early to make sure all the freight gets loaded."

"Phoebe?" I immediately feel a pang of jealousy, possessiveness. I hope that Strider didn't notice the crack in my voice.

"Yeah." Strider ruminates, then rolls down the window and spits. "Phoebe and Nan Reilly did all the provisioning. I just hope they bought some things that I like to eat."

Phoebe must be a woman who works at James and Jacobs. I settle down comfortably in my seat and look out the window. Fairbanks is so dull-looking: depressed old buildings and shopping malls. Some forest trees in the distance, and pink-blooming flowers along the side of the road. Strider doesn't talk, just chews and drives. I'm not much in the mood for conversation either. Mike and I went to a laundromat together to wash my new jeans so they wouldn't feel so stiff; but my red flannel shirt still shows the creases from where it was folded and pinned together.

Strider assures me that the person who fetches the truck will store my suitcase at the James and Jacobs office. I toss my head when I pass the polar bear this time: I'm part of an expeditionary team. It's going to my head—I'm swaggering all of a sudden, like someone who weighs more than I do. Like someone who can use a twelve-gauge shotgun (Mike Gavin has promised to teach me how).

And there is Mike and that is presumably Phoebe standing near him, bending over a coffin-sized wooden crate. I am pleased to note that she looks rather large and ungainly. When she stands up straight again, I see that she has the sort of body that was idealized in the nineteen forties and fifties. She's ample: voluptuous, and nearly as tall as Mike.

She has lots of silky thick dark-brown hair, nearly black; and pale skin—the sort they used to call peaches-and-cream. As we get closer I see that she has the slanted green eyes of a Modigliani painting. Her mouth is beautiful and full. She is standing very close to this man who has just become my lover.

Some blue-haired lady tourists with north-of-the-arctic-circle tote bags pause to gape at the serious-looking crates and boxes and guns. I hear them gabble, "Oh, they must be trappers or something!"

Phoebe sticks out her hand to greet me. "I'm Phoebe Gavin," she says.

Could she possibly be his sister? I know how stupid this is before I've finished thinking it. I spy the glint of a wedding ring on Phoebe's left hand. My own hand is as cold as ice suddenly. Hers feels dry and warm. She smiles at me. She has a narrow gap between her two front teeth, just like Catherine. I won't look at Mike Gavin. I won't. My God, his semen is still seeping out from between my legs. Hers too? How grotesque it all is. I have to spend the next eight weeks alone with these people.

Strider makes a gurgling, wheezing sound in his throat and coughs something up which he spits onto the floor. Oh, not alone! Strider will be there, too. "I'm going to go look after blue," he says.

"Are you okay?" says Phoebe to me. "I think you'd better sit down."

Mike puts his hand under my elbow. "Steady there," he says, as if I were a horse about to run away. I would love to kick him in his precious balls, but the whole airport's spinning.

"I'm fine," I say. "I guess I need to get something to eat." With my next breath I breathe in a promise to myself—I'm going to manage. How long can eight weeks last, after all? I smile unpleasantly at Phoebe—the same sicky fake smile I use for Dean Cooter. She's smarter than the Cootie, though. She looks—distressed. She looks like she saw the house of cards collapsing right inside me.

"The coffee shop's over there." She points. "Want me to go with you?"

"Thanks," I say, meaning no. Mike starts to say something, but I'm already walking down the lobby in front of all the ticket agents. I'm wondering what the hell Strider meant by looking after blue. Reminds me of licking one's wounds. Which is a pretty good description of the way I'm feeling now.

I really don't want to eat. I feel too sick to eat, so I just stroll around the cafeteria, pretending to look at the food that's for sale. Little boxes of cereal lined with foil so you can pour the milk right inside. Plastic-glazed sweetrolls. Glistening mounds of fried eggs and hash-brown potatoes still bearing the shape of the box they came in. I drink a glass of water and head for the ladies' room. I sit on the toilet seat staring at my wrist where my watch should be. He seemed so blue-eyed sweet and nice! A cornball, small town boy. Without guile. I use the toilet paper to wipe my tears. At the sink I wash my face and put my makeup on all over again. Thank God for makeup! Too bad that hats with veils went out of style.

We're aloft and I'm looking out the window. Phoebe's sitting between me and Mike. Strider's sitting by himself across the aisle, reading a paperback book with a picture of a woman warrior on the cover. They're all three drinking Bloody Marys—at eight-thirty in the morning.

"There won't be any alcohol at Darwin," says Phoebe to me when I ask the stewardess for orange juice, no ice.

"What about showers?"

Phoebe smiles like she hasn't quite understood. Then she laughs. "Showers! Oh, that's choice."

I smile back at her with all the self-confidence of someone who's just been intentionally witty. I guess that means there aren't any showers at Camp Darwin.

Phoebe turns to Mike and they talk about something I can't hear. A couple on the tour walk by, and the lady gives her husband a nudge. "Those are the trappers!" she whispers to him.

Down below, narrow, meandering streams cross and recross each other, forming braids of water and light in the low-slanting sun. Not a tree in sight (we're too far north for trees). The earth is pockmarked with strange pentagonal scars.

Phoebe taps my shoulder. "Do you see the ice lenses down there? They're caused by the strain of the earth shifting over the permafrost. The whole land is frozen just below the surface."

So even though it all looks so lush and green, everything's growing right on top of the ice: frozen not just for a season, but forever. It reminds me of Hans Christian Andersen's story of the Snow Queen. I never did buy into the idea of Santa Claus and a jolly frozen north. It was the image of the Snow Queen that stuck with me, her terrible mirror that broke in a thousand pieces, lodging in people's eyes and hearts. And everything they saw was ugly and evil, and their hearts turned to blocks of ice. Peg said that I cried for days after she read the story to me: I was so frightened by the idea of these invisible shards that could take our feelings away from us; that could leave us as cold and uncaring as snow (I was worried at the time that Peg and Denny might stop loving me). But it was my own heart I came to fear for: some dark growing coldness.

I blink back a tear and look out the window. There's absolutely nothing down there—empty land. The wilderness. The frozen heart.

The Eskimo town of Kotzebue is as far north as Alaska Airlines flies. As soon as we walk into the building, it's clear that something's wrong about this airport. It's too hot, first of all; and I notice that I'm swatting at mosquitoes, tiny ones buzzing around my face. Mike says over his shoulder, "Meet you back here in fifteen minutes," as he and Strider and Phoebe all head off in different directions. I head for the ladies' room. Ducking into one of the stalls, I'm just unbuttoning my pants when I notice that the partition seems to be missing between this stall and the next one: the doors looked normal on the outside, but here's the other toilet right next to me. Very funny. I'm sitting there feeling wildly constipated when one of the blue-haired ladies walks through the other door. "Hi there," I say for want of anything clever coming to mind.

She blinks her eyes behind thick glasses—the sort of glasses that people get after they've had cataract operations. "Oh, excuse me, dear!" She shuts the door quickly, and I can tell that she's standing there contemplating the two normal-looking doors, trying to take it in. She's wondering if this is a local custom—communal pee-pee—and whether her friend May Ellen will call her an old stick-in-the-mud prude for standing out there by the sinks—standing out there suffering—because she doesn't want to pull her panties down in front of a stranger.

I take pity on her and call out sweetly, "I'll be right out, M'am." I'm hoping there won't be outhouses at Darwin. The smell in outhouses makes me gag. I guess there'll be regular bathrooms. No one's said anything about it. My blue-haired lady looks so relieved and grateful as I come out. I can almost hear her thinking, "Such a nice clean girl, too!"

Besides the tour people, the airport is filled with Eskimos. They look just like they did in the geography books in elementary school: colorful parkas with wolf-skin ruffs; round Asiatic faces, and jaunty jet-black hair. They're marvelous looking, and they seem to all have come to meet the plane. I peek out the freight doors and see Eskimo men in pickup trucks, loading on crates and boxes and driving away. This doesn't make sense to me: Kotzebue is a tiny isolated dot on the map. There are no roads that lead in or out of the town. The blurb in the airline magazine said that Kotzebue is just a couple of miles from end to end, with the sea on one side and hundreds of miles of empty tundra stretching in every other direction.

Strider is walking up the ramp to the freight door, holding a doberman pinscher on a cinched-up lead. A group of giggling Eskimo children is following close at his heels. One of them pulls at the edge of Strider's denim shirt. "Excuse me, Mister." He and the other children are prettily dressed and look well cared-for.

Strider stops and turns around, looking very put out. "Yeah, what is it?"

The little boy holds his hand over his mouth and giggles, turning helplessly to the other children. A little girl pipes up. "He wants to know why you shaved off your dog's hair."

"Jesus!" says Strider, rolling his eyes. "I didn't shave him. That's the way he comes."

The children all stare at the dog, and I realize—of course—that this is Blue. "Doesn't he get cold?" asks the first little boy solemnly.

Strider reaches down and tousles the boy's hair. "Naw!" he says. "He don't live up here where it's so cold." He hands the lead to me. "Don't let it bite any of the kids," he says. "Blue gets nervous around kids. And when Blue gets nervous, he starts snappin'!" The children scatter.

I'm looking at Blue, wondering how I'm supposed to keep him from biting *me*. I walk him over to a big pile of crates marked "James and Jacobs" and sit down. Blue sits beside me, twitching his little stub of a tail, just like a cat does when it's nervous or feeling irritable. He yawns and and then snaps lethargically at some mosquitoes. I take note of his long white teeth. I'm wondering why I'm here and not in Berkeley drinking a *caffelatte* on the south edge of campus when all of a sudden Blue starts howling and straining at the lead. A truck drives up with an Eskimo man in a jean jacket behind the steering wheel and Mike and Strider in the front seat next to him.

They all jump out, the tailgate crashes down, and they begin loading on the crates, bags, and boxes. I try to help, but Strider says, "Just hold the dog, will you?"

Blue and I climb into the truck last: we sit in back with the freight. Blue keeps his gold-colored eyes on me the entire time, and I murmur things like, "Good dog! Nice doggie." He has a very doggish smell, and after I pat him, my hand smells doggish, too. Mike reaches around from the open window of the cab and hands me a paper bag containing a hot dog and some soggy chips. I can't believe it, but he clamps my fingers under his when he hands me the bag. I jerk my hand away and say, "Fat chance, creep!"; but my words tumble out of the truck and are lost on the empty tundra before they ever reach him. I tear off bits of the hot dog and feed them to Blue. Who knows when we'll eat again, though? I eat the last two bites myself, with Blue looking on resentfully.

Soon the road's gone and we're bumping along gravel and potholes and weeds until we get to a small airfield. Phoebe's standing there in front of an old, beat-up plane, talking with a man who looks as small as a jockey next to her. The little plane looks like something out of a World War II movie. The pilot looks like no sort of person I've ever seen before. His skin is an unearthly translucent pinkish ivory, like the skin of a newborn mouse or a baby bird. An army surplus cap hangs low over his eyes, which still shine out grayish blue. He laughs when he talks, and the skin around his eyes is crinkly.

"Tay, I'd like you to meet Bill," says Phoebe, "and this is his Otter" (touching the side of the plane). "Bill's the best bush pilot on the northwest coast. We're lucky to have him."

Bill gives my hand a warm squeeze. "I wouldn't think of trusting anyone else to land these two pretty ladies out on that God-forsaken excuse for a runway," he says, not to us, but to Mike and Strider. "Hey, I like your new pup, Strider!" Blue wags his tail with the ticktock of a metronome. "We'd better get this gear moved on. The wind's coming up."

Phoebe starts reading the labels on the crates and refers to a piece of paper she has on a clipboard. She kicks a box and the boys load it on. "Perishables!" she says. "This one goes. Tents and sleeping bags. Don't forget that one, Gav! What's this? Meat and veggies. Here's one, Bill!" I sit on a crated outboard motor that's been designated for the next trip out, letting on to Blue that I'm impressed despite my natural antipathies. How could he cheat on *her?* My God, she's like a queen. "Make sure you get the stove," (she points out each item with her pencil as she gives directions) "the propane, and the heater drum. Oops! Here's another box of perishables," and so on, until the plane is absolutely full except for the five seats, front and back. I follow everyone's example and pile in, forgetting even to take a last look at my feet on the ground. We buckle seatbelts. I'm in the back with Mike next to me, but I'm suddenly too scared to notice or mind. It hadn't occurred to me before that I've never been up in a small plane. (Oh, yes you have, my subconscious tells me, when you were about six years old, with Denny and a buddy of his, and the whole world turned bright red and you puked all over yourself and had to sit naked and shivering in a gas station bathroom while Denny rushed out to buy you some clean clothes.)

Bill revs up and the propellers spin dizzily. I think of the polar bear in the glass box at the Fairbanks terminal and ask in a shrill voice above the sound of the engines, "Is this where the polar bears live?"

Mike smiles. "Don't worry—you'll get to see bears, although maybe just grizzlies. It's probably too late for the polar bears—it all depends on what sort of ice year it is. The polar bears float out with the ice."

We make a mad, headlong rush to the end of the gravel strip and suddenly we're off the ground. The plane banks and turns north and then Bill cranes his head around to talk to us. "We had another mauling this spring," he shouts. "An Eskimo from Kivalina was out fishing and got separated from his buddies. This damn polar bear thought the guy looked like a good meal, and chased him down. He saw the bear coming and hightailed it for his boat—but the son-of-a-bitch dove right into the water and ripped the guy open. His friends saw it all happen, and finally shot the bear—not that it did their friend any good. He was dead meat when he hit the water." Bill nods and winks at me. "Pardon my French, Miss," he says.

"Poor bastard!" shouts Mike.

"Can't we find something else to talk about?" says Phoebe. "You guys are scaring Tay out of her shorts."

Mike grins at me.

"Unfortunate choice of words," I mutter; he squints his eyes and says "What?"; but I turn my head away.

I'm used to the idea of danger. I often think about it when I walk home from work in winter and the sun has already set and the sky is a bright electric blue in the west, but everywhere else it's dark. I'm afraid of lone men on the more unlighted stretches of College Avenue, of heavy footfalls behind me, and cars that follow slowly and then screech to a stop. Ever since Morgie and I stopped living together, I've been frightened sometimes when I know my neighbors are away and I wake up in the middle of the night with branches scraping at the window. Once I woke to see a face, like a wild creature, looking in at me, and I sat bolt upright and screamed. It disappeared into the night, and the police came, and dusted for fingerprints while I stood around in my nightgown. But I didn't believe in those fingerprints any more than I would have in the pawprints of a cheetah or a leopard or an evil spirit.

Fear is a presence for any single woman living in a city—like loneliness. I have my own ways of dealing with it, my own mumbo jumbo of superstitions, cautions, and lies. Two of my friends have been raped; I've been luckier. But this idea of being hunted down and eaten—of my humanity and womanhood being bypassed completely; of being considered as a bag of meat and bones: as food! I never worried about that in Berkeley.

Four

~~~~~~

"A pair of swans!" says Strider.

At first I think this is a call in some esoteric card game going on in the front seat, but then Bill dips the wing and descends swiftly, sending my stomach up to where my heart should be. I follow Strider's pointing arm and look out the window to see two white splotches, like crumpled sheets of typing paper, sail off below us in the distance.

"Oh, God," I say to Mike, just because he's sitting next to me. "I think I'm going to be sick." Usually when I think that, it happens. It would be poetic justice if I threw up all over Mike Gavin.

"Breathe in through your nose and out through your mouth," he says. "Slowly."

"Did you see them?" asks Strider, turning around from the co-pilot's seat. Then he smiles at me. "Hey, that's a nice shade of green you're wearing!"

"Oh, shut up, Percival," says Phoebe. "Leave her alone."

"Percival?" I ask, simultaneously emitting a tiny burp

that tastes of hot dogs. "Is that your first name, Strider?"

"Jesus, Gavin," says Strider. "Will you keep your wife under control?"

Well, I guess I didn't really believe that he had just one name, like a rock star or a medieval knight. Percival! It's fitting, really—Percival Strider. Oh, how the boy with that name must have suffered during elementary school and junior high! I'll bet he was one of those big boys who is afraid of fighting; who just wanted to be left alone. Who spent his school days sitting in the back two rows of the classroom with his chin tucked into the palm of his hand, waiting for the bell to ring. I'll bet he had a set of model trains at home—or some such thing—that kept him busy for hours and hours on his own. I can understand why such a person would be drawn to Alaska: ultimate left-aloneness. But what about Mike Gavin? What about Phoebe?

After what seems like about an hour of surreptitious burping and breathing slowly in through my nose and out through my mouth, I hazard looking out the windows again. To our right, the land is green, wet, and empty. Out to our left is the Chukchi Sea. On the other side of that is Siberia. I really can't imagine what I'm doing here, airsick and wedged between a man I've just made love to and his wife in a delapidated plane bound for someplace in the middle of nowhere.

Bill brings out a thermos from under his seat and offers us all hot black coffee from his cup. I'm worried about the acid from the coffee making things even worse for me, but I'm cold: I hold the cup and let the steam rise into my face. "Hey, the stewardess called in sick today, Miss, so we don't have our usual service." He laughs at his joke.

"You've made a big hit with Bill," says Phoebe, leaning

over Mike as she takes the cup from him, and resting a proprietary hand on his leg. "I've never seen him so talkative."

I can't help feeling aware of the warmth of Mike's leg next to mine. I stare out the window, shivering.

Bill is reading a paperback book. Every once in a while, he looks up to get his bearings. I'm wondering whether this is safe when two rusty oil drums come into view in the empty green below us. Several more appear, forming a straggly line that leads up to a huge garbage dump on a high spit of land, with a creek on one side and the ocean on the other. I reach forward and touch Bill's shoulder. "Who's dumping garbage out here?"

He turns and grins at me. "That's not garbage, Miss. That's the old army weather station. Those are antiques!" He puts his book down and starts a large circle over the junk pile with its rusted-out jeeps, five or six broken-down sheds, and wires flapping loosely in the wind.

"Are we landing?"

"That's been the gen'ral idea all along," says Bill.

"But I don't see a runway!"

"Well," says Bill. "It's an antique too. Sort of an old memory. Hold on to your hats, kids!"

We're dropping like a wounded duck, and I'm sorry all of a sudden that Peg and Denny never took me to church, because I sure wish I knew some prayers. I'm used to landings in seven-forty-sevens—smooth landings on smooth runways, when the passengers politely applaud. We hit the ground and then bounce into the air again: then hit and bounce and hit and bounce, like a stone skipping over the surface of a pond. Then the engines stop and we all stumble out of the plane into a breathless, overwhelming silence.

It's all over for me in a moment: I vomit onto the gravel, and when I raise my head again I feel tremendously better, despite the bad taste in my mouth and a little shakiness in the knees. Bill hands me a clean pocket handkerchief and I wonder if he has a wife at home who washed and ironed it for him. I can hear only two sounds: the lapping of waves and the rush of a creek. I take a step and the crunch of gravel is disproportionately loud, as if there are microphones hidden in the ground.

The silence roars in my ears, coming across the sea and hundreds of miles of empty tundra. I hear my heart beating. In a moment, I'm certain, I'll hear the blood surging through my veins and the subtle sound of my hair growing, and my fingernails. Strider lets Blue off his lead, and the dog frolics on the gravel, making it crackle and crunch until I want to put my hands over my ears.

The air is liquid and clear, like water seen through glass. As we stand there, the lavender sky breaks out into a sweat of color in three-hundred-and-sixty degrees around us, beginning with delicate veins of pale coral—the color of light shining through an earlobe. The sun hovers golden and fat as an egg yolk above the horizon.

"Well, let's unload," says Bill, and each syllable sparkles as it's caught by the silence and swallowed up. "It's almost midnight, and I've got to put the baby to bed." He pats the side of his plane. I reach up to touch it, too—the metal is cold.

This time I help. It feels good to touch things—familiar things like wood and nylon and canvas and metal. When the gear is all out on the ground, Bill hops back in the plane and starts the engines. I hold up the handkerchief. "I'll wash it and give it back to you later," I tell him. He winks at me.

Phoebe blows him a kiss. "See you with the next load of gear! Plan on eating a meal with us!" Bill touches his cap, then taxies around and roars down the gravel: miraculously, the plane rises into the sky, grows smaller and smaller, then pops like a bubble and disappears.

It comes to me all of a sudden that I'm stuck here. Mike hands me a dirty blue nylon bag. "Here's your tent, paleface." He laughs quietly, then walks over to Phoebe. "How about down by the creek?" She nods at him, and they begin to pick knowingly from the mound of stuff on the runway, filling their arms with gear and slinging backpacks over their shoulders. Then they both walk away from me into the distance that looks like darkness blown apart under a microscope, turning clear.

I feel like I've been dropped into an aquarium and told to breathe. I have to scrape my shoes in the gravel just to convince myself I haven't gone deaf. The background noise of traffic and electricity, the sound of civilization grinding its gears or simply sleeping—the background noise that is always there is gone. I'm staring out at the wet empty green and gray when all of a sudden I see a live thing moving: something dun-colored, like a piece of earth that's had life breathed into it. It's about the distance of a city block away from me, and just as I see it, it stops, and it's as if a wire has been stretched taut between us. I smell something ugly, like stale sweat, and I realize that the smell is coming from me: it's the smell of my fear. The thing I'm looking at can only be a grizzly bear.

I stand so still that the hair blowing around my face seems to make a racket. I think the breeze is blowing toward me (I hope the bear can't smell what I smell). My thoughts turn to the Eskimo straggler who was torn open with all his life spilling out of him. One animal to another, the bear and I stare at each other across the distance. I remember hearing somewhere that bears can't see very well, but they make up for it with their keen sense of smell. We are staring at each other, he with his nose and me with my eyes—and for a space of time long enough for me to grow considerably older, nothing exists in that landscape but me and that bear.

Then Phoebe's voice breaks in like a pair of wirecutters: "Tay, come on!" The bear turns and gallops away, his fur rolling and ruffling in his speed. I've never seen anything so fat move so quickly.

I find my carry-on bag in the pile on the runway and carry it, with my tent, toward the creek. As I pass Strider, I tell him, "I saw a bear." I point to where the bear stood, and then indicate the direction in which he ran.

Strider watches where I point, narrowing his eyes. I notice suddenly how much like a bear Strider is himself: I'll bet he can move fast when he has to. "Shit," he says, not to anyone in particular. He spits and trudges off to the runway. A minute later, he returns with a shotgun and scowls at me. I would like to tell him that it wasn't my fault I saw a bear, but before I can say anything, he crawls into his tent, holding the gun under his arm.

About halfway between the other two tents, I find a spot that looks fairly level, dump my stuff on the ground, kick some of the bigger stones aside, and ease the tent and the tent poles and stakes out of the stuff-sack. I unfold the tent, then stand there, staring at it all. I've been up since five-thirty; it must be past midnight now; I want to go to sleep. I'm not in the mood to build anything. The sky has continued changing colors, like paint on wet paper; the sunset keeps going on and on. I'm contemplating just wrapping myself in the tent when Phoebe walks up to me.

"Hey, you'll need this," she says. She puts an oversized sleeping-bag on the ground by my feet. "It's an incredibly warm bag—and we had it dry-cleaned."

She begins to set the tent-stakes, driving them into the ground expertly with the heel of her boot. "You know, it was me that wanted you to come along. Mike and Strider both like it better without women in the field—but, shit, I didn't want to be alone with them for eight weeks, without anyone to talk to, without anyone with any—polish." She tightens some ropes and the tent springs into life like a big beautiful butterfly, mostly blue, with panels of yellow and green. "Alaska's a wasteland for good talk—people like Strider read like they were watching television. And Mike's worse—he only reads if he can't avoid it."

Well, I was right about that, at least. Small comfort. I pick at the knot that holds the sleeping bag together, and look up into Phoebe's face for the first time since I met her at the airport.

I find myself wishing I were more like her. She strikes me as someone who never questions what she does, who has an inherent, almost regal, respect for her motives and desires. And I can tell suddenly as she meets my gaze that she lied: she would much rather be here by herself with Mike and Strider and Blue. The only thing I can do is foul things up for her. And she'll have to defend me, no matter how incompetent I am, just because I'm another woman. I look away from her, remembering how less than a day ago I was rolling on a chenille bedspread, naked, with her husband. I wonder if she guessed, back then, at the airport. "Why do you stay, then? I mean, if it's such a wasteland."

She looks at the tent admiringly. "I'll tell you about that

43

sometime." She looks back at me, but her face is different this time, softer, as if she's actually considering the possibility that we might become friends. "We have all summer."

As she walks off I call after her, "I know this sounds stupid, but where am I supposed to go the bathroom?"

Phoebe opens her jacket and brings out a small roll of toilet paper, tossing it to me through the clear air. "Just try to bury everything," she says. "It takes a long time for things to decompose up here. Years." As she walks away she turns a last time and adds, "Avoid the willows down by the creek—you don't want to run into any bears where the country's not open."

I walk until the land dips down, affording some privacy, and scrape a shallow hole in the gravelly ground with my shoe. I can still see the bright nylon banners of our tents on the crest of the hill. What did Phoebe mean by willows? I don't see any trees down by the creek or anywhere else. Squatting, I look out over the creek and the gray-green land to where it meets the sky. The watery sun balances on the horizon like a gold coin.

In Berkeley, I have a Sunday morning ritual. I set the alarm for six o'clock, as usual. When it wakes me, I turn it off and go back to sleep just for the pleasure of ignoring it. I sleep until my neighbor, Sam, who works at the Bread Garden, rings my doorbell at about eight-thirty. I throw on my bathrobe and pick up the five dollars and fifty cents I've set out on the kitchen table the night before. I hand Sam the money, and he hands me the white waxy bag filled with almond croissants. Then I put the kettle on and grind some coffee beans. I pour boiling water through the empty filter first to leach out chemicals from the paper and to warm the cup—my favorite one is a cream-colored ceramic mug with a scene from Beatrix Potter on it (Morgie and I had matching bunny cups). I swirl the water around and empty it into the sink. Then I shake the ground coffee into the filter, brushing out the last bits that cleave to the grinder; and pour the boiling water over again. The moistened grounds smell a little like skunk—but it is a smell I've grown to love. I drink the coffee black, because I don't have a milk steamer—and, anyway, *caffelatte* is a pleasure I reserve for cafes. I sit at the table in my robe and slippers and sip my coffee and eat an almond croissant, still warm from the bakery. Sometimes, in winter, I bring my coffee and croissant into bed with me.

I'm awake now. It wasn't the alarm clock that woke me, or the doorbell, or the kettle. Above me and all around me is a stained glass window, blue and yellow and green. I'm naked and lying in flannel, sweating just a little. At first, it seems that I am inside an oven; and then I remember that I'm inside a tent. I wonder what time it is. I rummage in my bag and put on fresh panties and wipe my face off with astringent and rub the crusts of sleep from my eyes. I would love to brush my teeth. I unzip the tent-flap and step out into the sparkling blue sky and fresh wind, and walk off to my place of the night before and pee. It's cold and I pull my pants up in a hurry, looking around me. I don't see anyone else, but then I hear Blue barking, and follow the sound down to the beach, where Phoebe, Mike, and Strider are huddled in a little knot near the surf, studying an array of objects spread out on top of a rusty oil drum.

"Mornin'!" says Mike, smiling at me. I can see now that it's just a habit of his to make his eyes sparkle. Type two: the cheat. Tight pants syndrome. His jeans *aren't* tight, not particularly: but his mental ones are. Every halfway decently attractive woman he meets is a tester: he sticks it in to make sure it's still working. She tells him he's the best ever. He pulls up his pants and gets on with the rest of his life: with his work and Phoebe. It's like going to the gas station, or going to the dentist every six months, or taking a shower every couple of days—but much more fun.

"Princess Grace decided to get up," says Strider.

I don't feel much like a princess. I feel an urgent need to either get some toothpaste or some coffee into my mouth.

"You're one to talk," says Phoebe. Turning to me, she adds, "Strider's famous for sleeping late. No one who knows him ever calls before one o'clock in the afternoon."

"Hell," says Mike. "No one calls Strider anyway."

Strider continues in his examination of the objects on the oil drum, handling them with surprising delicacy for such a big man. "What's this belong to?" he says to Mike, holding a small bone in the air.

"*I* know. What about you, Feeble? You're the bone expert."

"I'll feeble you. It's the scapula from someone who doesn't have much of an arm. Must be—" She takes the bone away from Strider and turns it round several ways. "Must be from a seal." Then she hands it to me. It's warm from the sunlight and smooth as the inside of an almond shell. It doesn't seem to have ever been part of anything else.

Mike picks up a paper-thin skull with some other tiny

hollow bones attached to it. "Know what this is?" he asks me.

"Where'd all this stuff come from, anyway?" I ask.

"Strider went beachcombing. Don't you want to guess?"

I stare at the hollow eye sockets. "A bird?"

"Right," drawls Mike. "I told you, Strider."

Strider picks up the skeleton of another bird with bits of leathery flesh and feathers still clinging to its wings. "This is a kittiwake killed by a gyrfalcon. The kittiwake was a year-old bird."

I stare at the animal wreckage, wondering how he can tell; then stare at Strider. I don't think that anyone's going to ask me about Pre-Raphaelite paintings here; or even about typewriters.

"He's just showing off," says Phoebe. "You'll be able to tell a gyr-kill yourself in a few weeks. Not that anyone knows as much as Percival."

"Fuck you, Phoebe."

"Fuck yourself, Strider. You want some coffee, Tay?"

I feel like a dwarf next to Phoebe as we walk up to the landing strip together, where a Coleman stove has been set up with a steaming tin pot of coffee and grounds sitting on top of it. Phoebe pours some of the muddy liquid into a cup for me. "Sugar?" I taste it: essence of skunk, overcooked. Phoebe points to a box of sugar and an open package of biscuits on the gravel. She nudges the box with her shoe and a ground squirrel runs out of it, causing me to jump. Then she smiles at me, seeming to apologize both for the coffee and the squirrel.

"Not what you're used to, I guess."

"Oh, it's fine, Phoebe. I was dying for some coffee."

I'm so sorry that I had sex with her husband—I wish I could undo what happened. But, then, if it hadn't been for Mike, I probably would never have agreed to come along. No—I would have turned right around and headed back to Berkeley. And would have missed that sunset last night. And that bear. And the sound of the naked world, the way a baby must hear it when it's first born.

Five

~~~~~~~~~~~~~~~~~~~~~~~~~~~

Phoebe pours herself a cup of coffee and dips a biscuit in it. We both sit cross-legged on the gravel. "The next few days are going to be hard, Tay. We've got to get a few of the sheds cleaned up right away while this weather holds; and they're in worse shape this year than ever. I guess some hunters camped out in the big one for a few months."

"They made a mess?"

"They left shit and rotting caribou meat inside. Mike's already gotten rid of the worst of it with a shovel."

I wave at a few mosquitoes in front of my face. "We're going to *sleep* in there?"

"No—that one's the kitchen. It's got a sink."

"There's plumbing?"

"Well, there's plumbing, I guess; but there's no running water. It's uh, it's really just a sink. It drains out into a bucket. Can you cook?"

I don't want to seem show-offy, so I just say to Phoebe, "Oh, I can cook a little."

She looks disappointed. "I was hoping you really *liked* to cook.

"I do, actually."

"Oh, don't worry about it. We'll all share the cooking." Mike and Strider walk by carrying a broom and a shovel, and disappear into the closest shed. "Grab a bucket," says Phoebe. "We might as well get started."

The buckets are plastic adhesive compound containers with wire bales. We walk down a gravel bank, slipping and sliding, to the creek, which flows down one long side of the isthmus that serves as a perch for our camp; on the other side of the isthmus is the sea. When we reach the shore of the creek, I step in mud up to my ankle: my new gray-and-white running shoes, compliments of James and Jacobs.

Phoebe smiles when I curse, for the first time, in front of her. "You might as well just lie down, roll around in it, and get it over with if it's going to bother you every time you get a little dirty."

"I'm going to have a hard time providing that polish you wanted at this rate."

"Look," says Phoebe. "I didn't mean I expected us to act like we were at a garden party. We're in the field, for God's sake." She walks out on a spit of gravel and dips her bucket into the stream, filling it about three-quarters full; then starts back up the slope.

I dip my muddy shoe into the stream to wash it off, then jump back with a gasp as something bites hard into my foot. The water is bone-cracking cold.

I fill my bucket, taking care to keep my hands dry; and struggle back up the slope of loose rocks and weeds, holding the full bucket as far away from me as my strength allows. More of the icy water sloshes over my pants and my shoes; my right shoe is sucking with a sensation I haven't remembered since childhood. Chessie Parker and I wore our tennis shoes into the lake at summer camp because we didn't like the slimy feeling of the moss at the bottom. It was deliciously unpleasant when Chessie and I walked back to the campground in our squishy tennis shoes, as if we'd been transformed by the water into some new sort of amphibious creature. When we took our shoes off, our toes were pale, wrinkled worms. We would put our feet together to experience the sensation of one cold, clammy thing touching another.

By the time I reach the gravel strip again, I'm in a sweat from the effort. Phoebe has amassed a pile of sponges, disinfectant, rubber gloves, and cleanser. We carry these and our full buckets to the first shed, up some wooden steps, and then through a storm door into a dark vestibule with coat hooks on the wall.

Everything is uniformly painted in gray, peeling paint. Phoebe opens a second door and we are inside the shed: a large room, dark, windows boarded up, terrible stink inside. Mike is ripping off the boards with a crowbar: as light seeps in, the gray walls bloom with all the colors of the filth that encrusts them. It's like being inside a giant angular toilet bowl that has never been cleaned.

Phoebe puts on gloves and pours disinfectant into her bucket. I say in a low voice to her, "Wouldn't it be nicer just to sleep in our tents?" But the room has fabulous acoustics—not unlike a tiled bathroom—and Strider and Mike both stop what they're doing to laugh at me.

Phoebe puts a gloved hand on my arm. "This weather's just a fluke, Tay. When the next storm blows in, you'll be real happy to be inside one of these sheds."

I have my doubts, but put on my gloves nonetheless and dip a large, salmon-colored sponge in the bucket of disinfectant. I guess I was a little off in my image of an X-ray technician: hospital orderly is more like it. I sponge off a strip of wall spattered with what looks like vomit and spaghetti sauce. After the third swipe and squeeze, the pristine creek water already looks gray. Strider is fitting together a stovepipe for an oil heater while Mike continues to wrench out the boards covering the windows. I'm grateful for the fresh air, as the smell of disinfectant mixed with the smell of whatever is on the walls is making me feel queasy.

"Never thought, I'll betcha, that you'd fly two thousand miles to clean up some Eskimo hunter's shit and puke," says Strider.

I remember, briefly, my fantasy of wearing furs and mushing a team of sled dogs. "Oh, I wouldn't have missed this for the world, Percival!" I smile at him without showing my teeth: a lip smile.

"Phoebe," he says. "I could murder you."

"What did I do?" she says, reaching up as far as she can on the wall with her sponge, not bothering to turn around to face him.

Strider mutters something down the stovepipe—it sounds pretty dirty.

"Watch what you say to my wife," says Mike.

"I wasn't talkin' to her," says Strider.

"Yeah, well, anyway, if you say something really nasty, I want to hear it. You come up with a good turn of phrase now and then."

"God, Gavin, you really are an asshole," says Strider.

"And Strider, you are a man of great perception," I add.

Mike stands poised with the crowbar in midair and looks at me with surprise. "What did *I* do?"

Phoebe turns and looks at him. "Yeah, what *did* you do?"

Suddenly this seems like a scene from *Cosi Fan Tutti*. I wonder, with some retention of breath, what Mike is going to do to wriggle out of this one.

With all the showmanship of a conjurer, he smiles winsomely, looking at each of us in turn. Then he sets down the crowbar and pats his breast pocket. I watch with a sort of disgusted admiration: Mike Gavin is the type of man who will always come out smelling like a rose, no matter how unsavory his actions have been. He's a naughty choirboy who gives pleasure to the person—no doubt, usually a woman—who forgives him.

Out of the pocket comes a little plastic bag of marijuana cigarettes. Oh, I know all about these things—I couldn't very much help it, growing up in Berkeley when I did.

"I was going to save this treat for later, children. But since you've all been so good . . ."

"Shit, Gavin," complains Strider. "We're never going to get done if we smoke that stuff. And the weather's changing—I can feel it."

"Trust me, Strider. This is going to improve our labor productivity, not make it worse." I look over at Phoebe to see whether she has fallen for it, and all I can see in her face is relief. She doesn't want, ever, *not* to be able to forgive him; she would really rather not know about his infractions, because there would have to be a scene, and I have a sense that Phoebe hates scenes—and I'll bet that Mike does, too. He lights a wooden matchstick with a flick of his thumbnail, and then sucks on a joint, passing it to Phoebe. She inhales, then passes it on to me. What the hell, I think: this is just the perfect sort of work to do stoned. I breathe in deeply, then cough, hard and long: it's been ages since I've smoked marijuana. Strider waves the joint away from him the first time around, but accepts some on the second round. He smokes delicately, holding the cigarette dead-center between his lips and puffing in.

I swipe at the wall with the obsessive curiosity that comes with dope: that makes you want to do something again just to reexperience its peculiar fascination, whether it's tasting food, or kissing, or doing some normally repellant and repetitive task such as the one we're doing now. After a while, I notice that the water in my bucket is a thick murky soup of filth: I walk outside with it and dump it onto the gravel runway, where it makes a nice hissing sound. Then I walk down the slippery talus to the creek, staying on the gravel and avoiding the mud this time.

Out on the end of the spit, I dip the bucket, feeling the weight of the stream tug along my arm all the way up to my shoulder. The air feels good in my lungs: fresh and clean. The sky is bright blue and I wonder what it is that made Strider sense a coming change in the weather. The sky is as illegible to me as the remnants of the bird that Strider identified. I've never learned to read the language of weather and sky, beyond the more obvious signals. The air down near the creek is relatively still, but when I climb over the top of the bank, the breeze falls all over me, playing with my hair and making me shiver with its chill.

It's much warmer, albeit smellier, inside the building. I set my bucket down by Phoebe's. Dope, like alcohol, loosens up something inside me and makes the insides of my thighs ache just a little, and my feet ticklish. Once in a while, out of the corner of my eye, I catch a glance of Mike looking so fit and attractive in his jean shirt with the sleeves rolled up: he's rinsing off the wall after Phoebe and I get through washing. We're all sloshing around in about half an inch of water that's slowly seeping down through a drain in the floor. Strider's got the stove built and is lying on a palette underneath it, trying to get the stove fired up. Then that other thing happens that happens when I smoke dope: I feel hungry. Oh, tremendously hungry.

I decide to show a little discipline, and not to think about food and not to think about Mike, but just to concentrate on stripping away all the colors down to the white wall that's hiding underneath. To strip away more and more with long swipes of my sponge. It's similar to a trick I use when I can't fall asleep at night: I think of a paint-roller dipped in the blackest black pulling its shade of colorlessness over everything. Whatever image I have, whomever I'm thinking of, the indifferent roller paints over it, paints it out, until there is only the tiniest strip of brightness showing through, like light showing under a door. And then the paint rolls over the last fragment until there is only darkness left, darkness and sleep.

Dear Morgie,

Oh, dear Morgie! You will never guess, not in a million years, whence I write you. Not from Fairbanks, dreary town of shopping malls and urban drunks. No! I am sitting in a military-style shed on the same latitude as Siberia, but on the other side of the Chukchi Sea, in the veritable middle of nowhere!

I can't possibly explain how I got here, not in detail. The story is as complicated and corny as the plot of one of your beloved operas. Suffice it to say that it was a case of romantic deception. And I am here, in this place without radio or telephone or post boxes or even roads, with an incomplete deck of Tarot cards: the

Trickster, the Clown, and the Queen. Are there such characters in the Tarot, Morgie? I remember the Trickster, certainly—but the others are hazier in my mind. Reading over this, I'm wondering if you think at this point that I'm simply playing with an incomplete deck: it does sound a bit like mad raving. The thing is, I'm not even sure how I'll mail this to you. A bush pilot, Bill, is supposed to bring in more of our supplies, but it started raining last night: we had exactly one day of fine weather, and I can't tell you how gray the atmosphere can be inside a gray-painted military shed on a gray day in the Arctic. Strider and I—he's the Clown, a sullen clown: or is there a Bear? Anyway, Strider and I fought over this room, if you can call it a room. Oh, we flipped a coin, like civilized people, but Strider was so inarticulately angry when he lost that he proceeded to tear apart the other half of the shed we're sharing: literally, he tore an old water heater and pipes out of the wall and threw them out the window! I thought that a bomb had exploded outside. It's all because my "room" has a homemade woodburning stove—what looks like a giant rusted-out sardine can with a crooked chimney. I went to great pains to gather driftwood for my coveted fireplace, only to find that it doesn't draw for beans, and sends billows of smoke into the room before extinguishing any fire I've managed to coax out of the wood. I used up my entire ration of matches and have had to cadge some from the supply in the kitchen. Oh, the kitchen is another shed, across from ours, where some Eskimo hunters holed up last winter and never bothered to attend to their personal needs outside—and they seem to have been sick to boot. We all smoked dope and cleaned up the mess and by the time we were finished—it took days!—the place had a sort of homey feel to it. Oh, home is where the heart is—or perhaps it's where the food is! These Tarot people are scientists—at least, the Bear and the Trickster are; the Queen is sort of a learned amateur (she's married to the Trickster, in case you haven't guessed).

One funny aside to all this: Do you know how strange an object a coin becomes when there's nothing to spend it on? Oh, I guess you do—like those funny foreign coins we all brought back from Europe. Useless! Not one tad of what I know about is useful here. One tad, perhaps: cooking. Apart from that, I'm the most miserable sort of ungifted drone. I don't have a clear idea yet of what the work is that's supposed to be done up here this summer—surely, it's something other than cleaning up after untidy Eskimos. But whatever it is—something having to do with counting birds—can't happen when the weather's bad, because we're supposed to go out in little rubber boats on that roiling Chukchi Sea. Send Dramamine! For this they're paying me twenty-two hundred a month. You'll appreciate this, Morgan-my-fay. I wanted to decorate my room, so I found half of an old weather-beaten oak toilet seat cover—there's an untold amount of junk all over the place here—and built a little brace underneath it, and stuck a candle in a bottletop in front of a tiny pocket mirror on top of it: and this tiny half-round shelf is my "vanity," where I can see exactly one eye at a time. World without mirrors! In the kitchen we have a jagged piece of broken mirror in front of which we all take turns flossing our teeth or taking surreptitious looks at the ravages of time upon our nearly middle-aged faces.

There were hints of tremendous, heart-stopping beauty when I first arrived here: a panoramic sunset that melted over the course of several hours into a sunrise, and all happening three-hundred-and-sixty degrees around us. But then the storm came, and everything is gray and couldn't be drearier. The kitchen has an oil heater which overheats it: so the choice is to sit in there drinking endless cups of Swiss Miss, playing pinochle with those living, steaming embodiments of the cards; or sitting in my room, shivering and hunkered up with one of the six—count them, six—paperback novels that Phoebe and I brought out between the two of us. Fortunately, Phoebe has good taste in books. Phoebe, in short, seems to be able to do everything: works harder than anyone, knows how to build just about anything, is perfectly gorgeous, and keeps surprising me with things like being able to speak French.

Well, my dear, this has gone beyond all lengths of propriety— and I suppose I had better ration my paper as much as anything else. I will seal this up and scour the skies for an airplane. Please send love to Peg and Denny; and only tell them what they might find amusing. Don't send out the Mounties—I really will be all right if I can stand the damp and the boredom for eight weeks. When I get back to the U, I'm going to spend all my time in the lovely third-floor bathroom with all that gorgeous hot running water. I'll move my typewriter in there, and the Cootie will have to speak to me through the door.

Write to me c/o the James and Jacobs address I gave you! They'll send in mail with our next supply of food. Much love,

Tay

Six

Five days here, and the quiet seems to have bored into me, eating away at the noise and glitter that have always been so much a part of my life—or at least as far back as when I began to try to be charming. No makeup (how ridiculous it would be!); no satchel full of all those things I thought necessary. Just blue jeans and a knife in my pocket. Chitchat floats away unanswered here. At first I felt rebuffed; and then it began to seem that my companions were trying to get me to listen to something that all my small talk and flirtation did its best to drown out: something that the landscape itself is trying to say.

Blue is my walking companion. I walk out into the rain and wind because it's driving me crazy sitting inside. Our sheds are on a hill on a long spit of land: down on one side, past the runway, is Ogoturuk Creek, curving all the way around the spit and finally to the sea. We can see the Chukchi from our west-facing windows: imperfectly through the plastic that Mike stretched over the wooden frames. But it's there, in the moments when the sky

clears—a leaden, frozen gray. When rain obscures our
view out the windows, we can still hear the sea, crashing
up on our long stretch of shingle beach, hissing as it
leaches back through the small, smooth stones. The noise
of the sea is constant. We heard it more faintly from our
tents, where the clear rushing of Ogoturuk was loudest;
but now, settled into our two sleeping sheds, the waves
are the last thing we hear as we fall asleep in the thin gray
twilight, and the sound that finally rouses us from our
dreams.

Phoebe and I go out to the runway in our rain parkas and
lift up the tarp that covers the remaining crates and boxes.
"This one!" she says to me, shouting through the wind.
We haul the crate out and carry it back to the kitchen. She
pries the lid off with a hammer. Inside, in two neat rows,
are frozen packets of meat and chicken from Safeway.
Phoebe selects four white bags containing half-thawed
Cornish game hens; we carry the remaining packets of
meat out to a hole in the ground that Strider has dug just
north of the kitchen and covered with a caribou skin,
half-tanned but discarded by an Eskimo hunter. This hole
is "the cooler," and perhaps because of the dead animal
presiding over it, and the dead animals inside, it is a
loathsome place. The permafrost of the earth itself will
keep our meats cold. Phoebe and I lower the clean white
packets into their grave. The hole seems to have its own
darkness around it: in its shadow, Phoebe's skin looks
particularly pale to me, dead-white and colorless; and our
hands on the packets of meat look like the hands of
crones. As she stows the last packet Phoebe touches my
hand with hers. "Are you cold?" she asks me, laughing

and showing her white teeth; and it is as if death has touched me. I think of Catherine touching my hand, how she said, *Courage*. As we walk back to the kitchen, I touch my cheek just to make sure I still have the warmth of life in me. My cheek is warm, but my hand smells of earth and ice and the grave.

"Would you like me to make a marinade?" I ask Phoebe when we get back to the Cornish hens.

She smiles at me. "Sure. Make some coleslaw, too. There's a couple of cabbages in that box over there and a jar of mayonnaise."

I divide the cabbage into quarters, and shred it with the large blade of my Swiss army knife. Mike and Strider gather driftwood and any other trashy wood they can find, as long as it's not coated with creosote, and build a fire just outside the kitchen. Phoebe finds a refrigerator rack in the junk pile and we use it for a grill. It has stopped raining for the moment, although the sky looks ominous— all dark gray, as if night were falling. Only I know as well as anyone else that the next nightfall is at least two months away.

I've rolled the little chickens around in some oil and cider vinegar and black pepper and powdered ginger— whatever I could find—and they browned up nicely on the hot grill. Mike threw some whole potatoes in the coals and we ate them hot and buttered for dessert. It all tastes so good, sitting out here in the cold twilight with our rain parkas on, eating off paper plates with rusty forks and our pocket knives. Maybe it has something to do with being hungry—really hungry (we've been working on the kitchen and our sleeping sheds since mid-morning—I think it must be, oh, way after the normal sort of dinner-time: ten or so). I am leaning back in my folding aluminum chair, gazing into the coals. "This beats some pretty expensive meals I've had."

"If you count the shipping costs," says Mike, "this little meal was probably the most expensive one you've ever eaten."

A drop of water hisses on the grill. The sky looks the same, but out over the Chukchi I can see a yellow-brown cloud as evil-looking as a swarm of insects. I guess it's a rain squall. The drops start falling harder and I put up the hood of my parka, ready for my sleeping bag.

Phoebe's voice breaks through the sound of waves and steam and fire. Her voice is as one would expect it to be: sonorous and expressive of a deep, relaxed self-confidence. "Well, now that we've had some food and some rest, maybe we should get the boats put together."

I smile at her joke, and have no wish to make any sound at all: next to Phoebe's voice, my own sounds like a tense, vibrating reed. I am content to listen to her, to enjoy my satiety, to anticipate the soft flannel lining of my sleeping bag. But suddenly I find that I'm sitting alone at the fire. Mike, Strider, and Phoebe are all rummaging around under the tarp on the runway. I walk over to them, squinting through the rain which is falling steadily now. "What time is it, anyway?" I am hoping that somebody will see the logic of going to bed.

Mike glances at his watch and says "Ten-thirty," then continues rummaging. He starts flinging out hip-boots and bright orange life preservers. Phoebe is changing her shoes, right out there on the runway. After she has her waders on, she slips the shapeless khaki rain cagoule over her head, covering her braided hair, her breasts, her waist, so that all that's left is the small oval of her face beneath her woolen watch cap. "You and I can build the thirteen-footer," she says next to my ear in the rain. "Better get your gear on."

Each drop of rain stings when it hits my face or hands: it's cold; it cuts like an icicle. I put on my hip boots just to be cooperative: when the time comes—*if* the time comes to launch boats, I'll simply wave and say *bon voyage*. I do have limits. It doesn't take an expert to see that a storm is blowing in. Strider told me about how cold the Chukchi is—with great relish, over a pinochle game. It's colder than Ogoturuk Creek where I dipped my foot in the water and thought I was being attacked by piranhas: it only takes two minutes in that water before hypothermia sets in. There's no warming up once you get that cold. Phoebe told Strider to hush up when he was telling his story. Oh, but Phoebe doesn't seem to care about being tired, or hungry, or cold, or even about death.

She's shouting at me through the rain that whips around us now like ropes, "Come stand here on the floorboards, Tay! Help me with these stringers!" I obey her, stiff and stupid and shapeless in my foul-weather gear. I look around at the others while I'm jumping up and down on a foot pump, driving air into the pontoons: Mike and Strider look like rain-soaked trees, bending and blowing. It suddenly doesn't seem to matter who we are and what we have or haven't done together: we've become primitive in the cold, scurrying members of a small, isolated tribe. I try to picture myself and Mike in the Miner's Dream Motor Lodge, two people making love in the shower and artfully having sex on a white chenille bedspread. It seems like a scene from a movie, perfectly imagined but unreal. The images are from a forgotten world: shower, bedspread, white chenille. In three days the reality of all my memories has melted away. Silk blouses, high-heeled pumps, shoulder pads: it all seems unspeakably ridiculous. What is real now is the rain, the wind, the colorless landscape.

Phoebe masterminds the assembly of the puzzle-like floorboards, snapping them into place. The boat has changed from a flat thing in a box to a bloated, beached whale. Mike is shouting at us from the other boat—the larger one. Bill hasn't returned yet with the rest of our supplies, which apparently includes two smaller outboard engines; but the really large engine came out with us in our first load of gear.

My letter to Morgie is still sitting in its envelope, neatly stamped and addressed, on my little shelf underneath the candle. I can hear Blue howling from inside the kitchen.

"Let's see if this baby floats!" says Mike. He's pulling gloves out of his pockets, just like a magician, one after the other: cotton work gloves and bright orange rubber ones. He has enough for all of us. The cotton ones go under the rubber ones. Each of us grabs one of the boat's rope handles, two on each side. I lift up on my handle, but nothing happens—you know that feeling when you try to lift something that's simply beyond your strength: it doesn't even budge. The others are lifting their handles and the boat is suspended, more or less, between us— except my corner is dragging over the gravel. "Come *on*, Tay!" says Strider. "Don't make a hole in the bottom of the frigging boat!"

I don't understand why everyone else is so much stronger than I am. I feel the sort of humiliation that I haven't felt since kindergarten, when I was a frail freckled girl who played with dolls and was afraid of the playground bully—a girl who stood head and shoulders above me and was such a dare-devil that she always had one arm or the other in a cast or a sling. She used her cast as a weapon and was the terror of the playground. Carol Lyman, her name was. I used to run and hide in the bathroom when I saw her coming. I remember crouching in the stall on top of the toilet so she wouldn't see my feet under the door, and she taunted, "Sissy, sissy, piss your pants and run to your mommy!" Sometimes she would crouch down and push the horrible cast in under the door. Once, in a moment of mindless panic, I did wet my pants, and had to wait in shame in the nurse's office while Peg drove down from the mountain to take me home. I wouldn't think, though, of telling my parents about Carol—such was her power over me.

I am pulling up on the rope handle as hard as I can. I feel like my arms are going to pull out of their sockets. Mike decides that one place in the bank is not as steep as the rest, and we start downhill there—and it's all we can do to keep the boat from getting away from us. Talus, even without a load that is sapping all your strength, is slippery stuff. I'm balancing on the boat as much as carrying it—every scrape of the rubber against the gravel sets my teeth on edge, and Strider is now muttering nonstop imprecations at me under his breath.

But as bad as it is, when we reach the edge of the creek I wish we had further to go. It's just what I was afraid of: they are shoving the boat nose-first into the water. They are wading in up to their knees, despite the rain, which is blowing even harder now. I step into the water tentatively, dubious about the insulating power of these boots—but they do seem to work. That's fine—I'll wait for them here. I'll wait for them standing in the water if they want me to.

"Hop in!" shouts Mike as he and the other two adeptly spring up over the pontoons, where they perch looking smug and accomplished. "Jump, damn it!" Mike shouts at me as I stand there thinking about the coldness of the Chukchi and about the heaviness of these boots, weighted with lead at the heel and toe. Wouldn't I just sink down like stone, never having made a thing of lasting value: not a sculpture, not a painting, not a book, not even a child.

I smile at Mike, remembering how he kissed my shoulder and then my forehead. It doesn't seem possible now: those two warm, dry people were not us. "Sexy" is not a concept that can exist in the wind and rain, in the icy coldness, with the crash of the Chukchi still reaching our ears. "I'm scared, Mike!" I shout at him, my voice straining to be heard above the furious weather. He and Strider are trying to keep the boat from catching in the current. They look like they're having a difficult time.

Phoebe reaches out her arm and I can see through the rain that she's smiling coaxingly, as one would smile at an animal or a small child. I see Carol Lyman all over again, that arm in its cast, chasing me across the playground.

Well, Peg's not around to pick me up, there's no bathroom to run to, and anyway I've about had it with these playground bullies. It's not often that one gets the chance to relive a moment in the past so that it comes out differently. I shout at Phoebe, "Don't patronize me!" and make a leap for the boat, flinging myself head first in all my waterproofed bulk over the closest pontoon. I can't seem to pull in my legs, which are hanging over the side, dripping and heavy and as out of control as if they belonged to somebody else. Strider gives me a thump backwards on the chest and I bob upright, gasping: my legs clump down onto the wooden floorboards.

"What were you saying?" says Phoebe to me. "I couldn't hear you."

"Never mind," I say, and I really do feel like crying. The boat catches in the current like a leaf, and we start floating, inexorably, toward the sea. Somehow I forgot that I promised myself not to come along. And here I am. In an instant, Darwin has completely disappeared.

In the camp, filled with decades of industrial castoffs and remnants of all the soldiers, whalers, hunters, and scientists who had passed through, there was a bogus sense of civilization. I forgot our bird's-eye view from the plane: that the junk pile is in the middle of nowhere. Phoebe looked large and strong at the camp: here she's as small and frail as I am; and so are Mike and Strider. We're four people in a rubber boat, mortal creatures with skin that can be bruised and scraped, long breakable fingers, bodies that can be violated in a thousand ways, bones that can be crunched by polar bears, organs that will fail in the black silent depths of the Chukchi Sea. Even Carol Lyman would be humbled here, minimized to a pitiful squirting of warm blood to a quickly beating rabbit's heart, a fluttering as short-lived as a hummingbird or a butterfly.

And suddenly I understand, and the knowledge spreads like a warm liquid inside me: I am going to die someday. Really die—complete end, no more chances. I look around me gulping the air, seeing the brightness of colors, feeling the warmth of my body inside my clothes, and I realize that it may happen soon; it may happen in just a few moments. Why haven't I ever realized it before? When I think of the time I've wasted; how I was waiting, waiting, and for what? For death by ice, by coldness, by numbness, by passivity.

I saw Granny MacElroy die—or I saw her just before she

died. Her lips were forming words that she couldn't pronounce anymore; her eyes looked out on a middle distance that didn't include any of us. And then, while she was sleeping, she died. But she was old! She had produced Denny and Uncle John; she had the satisfaction of settling money on each of her grandchildren. But that thing that visited Granny in the middle of the night—that icy cold thing that sucked out life, that blew it out like a candle: that thing isn't possibly for me, not yet. Oh, please God, not yet.

We float downstream toward the sea in silence. I hope to die quickly, without pain. I am sorry that I haven't told Peg and Denny how grateful I am for all they've done for me, for their unconditional love and trust and faith. I think about the pale pink bowl and how it shall always remain empty. I am sorry that I did not somehow steal Morgie's sperm from him and have his baby. I will go out of the world leaving nothing behind me, and it will be as if I had never lived.

We reach the delta where Ogoturuk spreads out to meet the crashing sea. The boat spins once before it sticks fast in the mud. Phoebe, Mike, and Strider hop out onto the sand. I follow with weak, wobbly knees. My clothes are soaked with sweat.

Phoebe studies the sky for a moment. "It's clearing. Maybe we can get out for a look at the colonies."

I hold my breath. "It's not clearing," says Strider. "This is the fucking eye of the storm."

I could kiss him, fat Strider, fat logical Strider, oh deliverer. I feel faint and feverish.

Mike is sniffing the air like an animal. "Strider's right, Feeble. Look out there to the northwest."

The fleshy pink of the sunset/sunrise is tinged a yellowy-brown. The air looks alive, dangerous, like a frayed wire. I feel a sudden burst of energy as we haul the boat up by its bowline and bury the anchor in the smooth stones of the beach just below our camp. Then I lie down on my back just where I am on the damp stones, crucified, exhausted.

After a moment, Phoebe clasps my hand and pulls me upright. "You looked pretty scared back there," she says.

I blink my eyes, still getting used to being alive. "Well, it's just that the Chukchi—and this boat, the storm. I thought you'd all gone crazy. That we were all going to drown."

"You have a vivid imagination," says Phoebe. "And Strider's been telling you too many stories. No one around here is interested in dying."

"But I don't understand. What's the big rush about getting out to these colonies?"

Phoebe gazes northward before looking back at me. "We've got a lot of work to get done. And every day we stay here, we're missing something that's happening out *there*. Everything happens fast during the summer here. It's—well, nature only has three warm months out of the whole year to get everything done: the mating, the egg-laying, the hatching, the fledging. Every day counts. Maybe you'll understand when you see the colonies. They have a certain smell: I can never remember that smell until I'm out there again. I guess some people hanker after the smell of chestnuts in Paris in the wintertime. I hanker after the smell of birds and damp grass and rotten cliffs overlooking the sea. I guess you really must think I'm crazy now."

"I don't know if you're crazy, Phoebe. But I sure don't understand you. I've never met anyone like you before. Or Mike. Or Strider, for that matter."

"Yeah, Alaska attracts sort of weird types, I guess. Doesn't it make you wonder about yourself?"

"Me?" I shrug my shoulders. I'm about to say that I'm only here temporarily, so the rule doesn't really apply; but then I catch Phoebe's glance and we both start laughing. We're walking by ourselves, where Strider and Mike can't hear us. "Aren't you ever afraid?" I ask her.

She looks serious. "I'm sometimes afraid I won't get to see the colonies again. Or be out in the field again. Mike talks about having kids some time, and I just can't imagine being tied down like that, having to stay near town, near day-care centers and shopping malls and all that. I'm sometimes afraid that I'm just too selfish to be a mother."

The sky has darkened again, and larger, colder drops begin to fall. We hear Blue howling when we stamp up to the storm door in our heavy waders. Mike and Strider are already inside, boiling water for hot chocolate.

When I finally crawl into my tent and strip off the last layer of clothes, I only have time to notice how horribly I stink before I fall asleep. 'I smell just like Blue,' I think to myself. 'Me!' But the down bag opens and accepts me anyway. My limbs grow dry and warm and heavy as something hewn from the rain-sodden earth itself. I dream—oddly, perversely—of the third-floor women's bathroom in McLaughlin Hall, recalling details that I never consciously noticed before—the rust-stained marble walls, the oak doors with dull metal hinges, the porcelain knobs on the sinks marked with H and C for hot and cold running water. In the dream there's a shower running and the bathroom is filling with steam. Granny MacElroy is sitting behind a little table by the door, like the old women who tend the public bathrooms in Spain; but she is nearly hidden behind a colorful stack of folded and freshly washed cotton bath towels. My eyes are stinging with tears as I say to her, "Granny, you're *not* dead!" and I put my arms around her gently, and pick her up like a baby. "Granny, you're as light as a leaf!" I tell her. 'It's those MacElroy bones,' I'm thinking. 'They're like bird-bones. They break too easily.'

Seven

In the morning—if it's still morning—I write a long letter to Peg and Denny, seal it up, and put it under my letter to Morgie. No sign of Bill yet. I'm too filthy to justify a clean pair of panties, and I wince as I put on my old soiled ones. My longjohns, as I pull them on, feel damp—but everything is. The new day is as dull and gray with rain as the one that came before it. After my pee behind one of the outbuildings, I crunch my way over the gravel to the kitchen, and burst in, famished.

Phoebe's reading a book at the kitchen table. Mike is in front of the stove flipping pancakes.

"Good mornin'," he says. Mike doesn't so much converse as insinuate. His good morning is loaded with innuendo: his eyes sparkle, he smiles, and laughs in a way that would be called giggling if a woman did it. I have no idea what all this is supposed to communicate.

"We're taking bets," says Phoebe without looking up from her book, "about whether Strider will make fifteen hours. Care to wager?"

"God," I say. "How long did *I* sleep?"

"Twelve." She puts her book face-down and I'm aware of her watching me as I pour coffee for myself. Mike hands me my plate (a sky-blue plastic one with a cigarette stain): one fried egg, sandwiched between four pancakes, smothered in syrup.

"Madame," he says in fake maitre d' style.

"There's some hot coffee," says Phoebe.

For a moment I forget human complications in the sheer enjoyment of my food. But when I'm done feeding, the room begins to feel hot and uncomfortable to me.

When we're alone, Phoebe and I can talk—*really* talk, in the same way that I and all my close women friends can talk (even though Phoebe and I are just starting out at this together). But when we're around Mike, the well of conversation goes dry. Women know how to talk to each other: but unless a man is very unusual (Morgie is one of those unusual men—and look at Morgie!), the pattern of talk changes when a man's around. It's like an interruption in the magnetic field. And that deep, soul-satisfying exchange becomes chatter—just the sort of meaningless yammering that men are so fond of deprecating. In our case, because we're both somehow conscious of what happens around Mike, our talk becomes something stiff and academic.

We discuss the book Phoebe's reading—it's Iris Murdoch's *The Sea, The Sea*. Phoebe says she likes Doris Lessing much more; and I tell her how angry *The Golden Notebook* made me—how betrayed I felt at the end when it turned out that the narrator was lying. And all the time we're talking, like two faculty wives at a tea party, my attention is divided, because some part of me is thinking about Mike. He can't talk about either author, because he

74

no doubt hasn't read them: but there is something in our situation that allows him to sit in his folding aluminum chair looking as fatuous as a bumblebee. And I'm certain that it's this physical possession thing: he has "done" both of us. There's a part of me that would like then and there to tell the truth to Phoebe; to get it all out into the open. But Mike knows I won't do that—I'm too fond of her. And yet, I feel a strong sense that Phoebe knows: knows and chooses not to know at the same time.

I came up here to the Arctic lured by a possible romance; but in a larger sense, I came because I hoped for some sort of transformation: something large and meaningful. Instead I feel the outside pressing me in: there's no long perspective at all—only the minutiae of our small and new relationships: weighing this against that, recording my impressions, and remaining, behind it all, the same. Cold, in a way; scientific.

"I've never been so dirty in my life," I announce. "I had no idea I could be so disgusting!" Maybe I want Phoebe to know that I don't need to appear attractive to Mike. But, at the same time, with a miserable twinge, I'm aware of calling attention to myself in the most personal, flirtatious sort of way.

"Ah," he says "You may reach new heights—"

"Or depths," interrupts Phoebe.

"The rest of the summer awaits you!"

"I don't plan on going for the rest of the summer without bathing—Jeez!" The smell of my body when I take off my clothes reminds me all too uncomfortably of the way Strider smelled when he picked me up at the airport. "Don't you bathe out here?" I ask Phoebe. "Sponge baths or something?"

"Oh, when I can't stand the smell anymore."

"Or *I* can't," says Mike. It strikes me as a particularly un-gallant remark—and Phoebe registers, just briefly, a hurt look: a sort of momentary glazing over of her eyes.

"Yeah," she says, bouncing back. "Men seem to be able to go a lot longer than women before they get offensive. One of nature's little injustices."

"Welcome to the animal kingdom, Miss MacElroy—a magic land where species are self-perfuming."

"You might not use that phrase if you were sitting any closer."

"It's a great way to ensure marital fidelity," Phoebe says, buried in her book again.

"Fidelity—shit! Chastity!" says Mike. "You're no per-fumerie yourself, Feeble."

Phoebe deliberately finishes reading the sentence she's reading—or pretends to; then closes her book and sets it down on the table. "I'm going for a walk," she says quietly, putting on her foul-weather gear of the night before. She clumps across the floor in her hip-waders and carefully closes the inner door; but then slams the outer one so hard that the coffee pot shakes on the table.

I look at Mike. He's not smiling or sparkling any more. His face looks tired. "You want some more pancakes?" he asks me.

"How can you talk about pancakes?" I can feel my face flushing, and the telltale splotches I get on my neck when I'm angry.

Mike walks over to me—so close that I can smell the warmth of him in the hot room.

I've begun to cry, but it's anger, not weakness—except he has no way of knowing that. He hasn't understood me at all. "You seem like a decent sort of person in all other ways." I look down at my shoes, then up into his face.

"How could you have done it, Mike? How could you have tricked me like that?"

He is staring out the window. I hear him swallow. "I was only being friendly, Tay. And you're a very attractive lady."

"But you're married."

He turns his face toward me again, and it's like standing under a heat-lamp. "Would you have done anything different if you'd known that back then?"

I'm about to say that I never would have gone to bed with him, and then I remember what it felt like, kissing him. Being kissed by him.

He saves me the embarrassment of my answer, the large 'I don't know' sticking in my throat like a pill not completely swallowed. "Maybe I didn't want to miss out on the experience," he says quietly.

Our eyes meet for a moment, but I can't look at him. "I'm going outside," I mumble, adding in a whisper, "It's too hot in here."

I can't believe that I've walked out from that nice warm fragrant kitchen into the freezing drizzle and rain. So that's what they call cabin fever! People go crazy when they're shut up together too long.

I walk down to the beach, looking for Phoebe. The wind is blowing off the water, and suddenly I smell something horrible: not anything as tame as dirtiness or sweat. This is the smell of death and decay.

Holding my nose, I scour the shoreline. And then I see it: something pale silvery gray and shiny; something very large, rocking back and forth in the surf. The only thing I can think of that would be so large is a whale. I can see Phoebe's figure crouching nearby, hunched over a length of rope and (as I get closer) a grappling hook. She looks up at me cheerfully. "I've got dibs on the jawbones!" she shouts at me above the crash of the waves.

I look out at the shimmering gray carcass, well along in the process of decay. "Be my guest!" I shout back at her. "But how are you going to get the whale to part with them?"

She pulls a hatchet out of her belt; I back away from her. "You've got to be kidding!"

"Have you ever seen the jawbones of a gray whale? They're some of the most beautiful bones there are. I'm going to use them as an arch over the front door to the house we're going to build next year." She gets back to her work of threading the rope, then squints up at me through the drizzle. The wind dies down for a moment, and the waves seem to fall more quietly. "Will you help me, Tay? I'd rather not ask any favors of Mike just now."

"Of course I will. I mean, I'll try—but it looks awfully heavy. If I had trouble just lifting one corner of that boat, I don't think I'll be much help moving a whale . . ."

"We'll let the waves help us." Emotional shadows pass deftly over Phoebe, as if all her light defies them. As she speaks, she finishes slipping about half the length of rope through the hook and then ties one end around my waist. "You know," she says, "I think you underestimate your own strength."

"Phoebe," I swallow, "I only weigh a hundred and fourteen pounds with my shoes on."

"It has very little to do with weight or size. Don't you know that, Tay? It's all a matter of balance—and timing!" She ties the other end of the rope to herself, makes a coil of the slack, and drapes it over her shoulder. "I'm going to get hold of the whale and then we'll fan out. Try to pull as the waves roll in. And if I fall in a hole or get knocked down or something, run up the beach—don't come in after me. Okay?'' She wades off into the surf as blithely as someone going off on a picnic.

I plant my feet on the ground in second position and try to concentrate, as I do in ballet class, on keeping my center of balance just above my hips, somewhere around my solar plexus. I watch with a sinking feeling of anxiety as the water rises higher and higher toward the top of Phoebe's boots. The rain and spray make it difficult to see, but I can just make out that she has fastened the hook somewhere— through the mouth?—and is wading back downshore of me, motioning for me to start moving backwards.

I lean backwards and we pull together in rhythm with the whale's rocking motion, clumsily at first, so that I'm sure that we'll never budge it an inch. Two women, no matter how much in rhythm with the waves, cannot move a whale. There it lies: intractable, huge, filthy, and phallic, the size of a large American car. I think, as I'm pulling, of mystical connections, of the forces that keep oceans and women in unconscious synchrony, moon to moon, tide to tide. I hold on to the rope with both hands, lean back with all my strength, and close my eyes.

I would like to believe that Phoebe's right: that all along I've underestimated my strength. I can imagine suddenly the sensation of tremendous strength: of strong arms and legs, of a deep sonorous voice. I strain with all my weight against the rope; I stumble. When I open my eyes and look down, I can see the progression of my footprints in the small wet rocks: quite to my surprise, we have hauled the whale about three feet closer inshore.

I look down the beach at Phoebe. "Just lean away from it!" she shouts through cupped hands; and then she runs like a savage, waving her hatchet and yelping, back out into the waves. She hacks away at the putrid blubber in a bath of salt spray, waves rolling in and breaking over her shoulders. It makes me think of *Moby Dick*—how there wasn't one single woman in that rich, complex feast of a novel, although the men themselves filled in the women's roles: Ishmael woke up in Queequeg's ambiguous embrace at The Spouter-Inn; the whalers sat round in the "Squeeze of the Hand" chapter enslimed and enshrined in their own homoerotic sensuality. And there's my Phoebe, hacking away with her hatchet, as mad and heroic as any of Melville's creations, up to her elbows in rotten flesh, up to the top of her boots in the sea.

And, of course, when she's seen in this light it seems that nothing of Mike's ungallant or downright deceitful behavior can ever touch her—not really. Phoebe is made of the stuff of myths and epic poems—Mike is a miserable sort of creature next to her, pitifully mortal and fallible. Like myself. Oh, I can appreciate Phoebe: I can worship her. But I can never aspire to be in her league.

She emerges from the curtain of spray like a soldier returning from the battlefield, dragging at her side the rough round arches of the jawbones like two slain animals, the rotten, stinking flesh still clinging to them. I move back involuntarily from the overwhelming odor as Phoebe comes close to me with her trophies.

"Oh, God, I'm sorry!" she pants, her hair plastered to her forehead and her clothes completely soaked with brine and blood. "This is the worst sort of stink, too. It stays on you for days. But aren't these beautiful?"

"Beautiful!" I parrot back at her, dumb with admiration. I only glance briefly at the grim spectacle of the jawbones. My eyes are all for Phoebe, for this grisly Venus rising up out of the sea.

"Well, just wait till we get them cleaned up! They have perfect lines—I'd rather have them than any old Greek statue." She carefully lays them down on the pebbles. The rain has stopped. Phoebe walks up and down the beach, picking up pieces of driftwood and throwing them into a pile. In a short time she has these smouldering, with a rusty black iron cauldron filled with seawater hissing over them. The jawbones only fit in part way, with the rest of their raw flags of flesh sticking out over the top of the water. Phoebe sits upwind of the flames, shivering. Her lips are blue. I half expect her to utter prophecies, like an oracle by her fire; but she simply says, more to herself than to me, "Just wait till Strider sees these. He'll be so jealous."

I coil the rope that we used to pull in the whale, and gather a few more pieces of wood to feed the fire. When it's clear that Phoebe intends to stay there, I back away quietly, filled with sudden intention.

The whale is with me as completely as if I had slept inside it. The smell is everywhere—on my hands, on my hair, on my clothes. I kick my way through one of the piles of junk and find a tin bucket. Half running with it up the hill and down the other side to the creek, I fill it with water and carry it into the kitchen where Mike and Strider are hunched over some maps.

"Jesus!" says Mike, blinking his eyes. "What have you been rolling in?"

"Whale funk." I light one of the burners and lift the bucket onto the stove. "As soon as this heats up, I'll be out of your hair."

"A cover will speed things up," says Strider, finding a large pie tin and placing it over the bucket.

While the water's heating, I gather together shampoo, a new kitchen sponge, soap, and my limp towel; and put plastic bags over my hands to lay out fresh underwear, longjohns, socks, and jeans. My clean clothes have a heavenly fragrance of civilization. When the water grows a lining of silver bubbles, I put on a pair of work gloves to carry the bucket down to the creek near my pile of soaps and clean clothes.

I unbutton my wool outer shirt and slip it off onto the ground. I suck in a long breath of air and lift my wool undershirt over my head. The wind bites into me. My tee shirt comes next: I throw it as far away from me as I can when I get the first whiff of the smell it's harboring. My skin breaks into gooseflesh. My hair is so oily that it doesn't even seem like my hair anymore: I comb my fingers through, kick off my shoes, then in a burst of determination, strip off my socks, slip out of my jeans, and fling off my panties and bra. I stand there electrified by the cold and faint with my stench.

I try the water in the bucket, but can't tell how hot it is: it's simply hotter than everything else, and a welcome reprieve from the cold wind. Soaping up the sponge I let out a cry at the first wet swipe across my body—followed by a lick of cold wind, it has the effect of sandpaper on my skin. I gulp more air and scrub at my arms, scrape at my armpits, my chest, my thighs. How it hurts! But the smell of soap begins to dominate over the smell of dead whale and old sweat and unwashed panties. I step into the bucket with both feet and scrub. I squat over the bucket and soap relentlessly. And finally I kneel, like a penitent, with the rough stones pressing their shapes into my knees, immersing my hair and using shampoo with abandon until it begins to foam. Then, thinking of Phoebe as she ran out to the whale brandishing her hatchet, I pour the whole bucket over me in a sudden rush of warmth; and run, shrieking and protesting like some crazed bacchante, straight into Ogoturuk's icy waters.

I bob up like a cork, but force myself down again into the cold, tossing my head from side to side, rinsing my hair, ridding myself of the accumulated stink of a week of work and other people's filth and the putridness of a whale that has been dead for over a year.

When I step, slow and heavily, out of the water, I can't even feel the sharp stones under my feet. The air is charged with warmth; the breeze is tropical, caressing. I dry off, noticing but not caring about the purple bruises on my legs. My mind is dull, sedated, as if I had swallowed a fistful of drugs or had just woken up from dreaming. My clean cotton clothes slip over me like silk.

I stand still, watching the stream—all this flow of water, unending except when winter freezes it. How can so much water flow into the sea without the sea spilling over? The other part of the cycle—the evaporation, the clouds blowing inland, the rain—seems so much slower, more ponderous: no match for this relentless abundance. And yet, somehow, there is a balance. Perhaps it's happening in a way I can't see inside—an unburdening, a balance; a thaw.

Eight

~~~~~~~~~~~~~

There's no sound of rain as I wake up this morning. Someone is banging on the wall below my window. "We're going to launch the boat!" shouts Phoebe. "We're leaving in half an hour!"

I dress in my clean clothes, so glad that I've bathed, and trundle into the kitchen. Things look chaotic: boxes of food strewn all over the table and floor; equipment and packs and bundles everywhere. Even Strider is awake and dressed, blowing on a cup of coffee and writing in a small yellow notebook. Mike hands me a bowl of oatmeal. I look into his eyes, one mortal to another, nod, and say thank you.

Phoebe takes a pencil out of her mouth to talk to me. "When you're done eating, Tay, pack some extra socks and jeans, and put on your warmest sweater. We're going out to Colony IV."

I smile up from my cereal. "Okey dokey." Somehow, after Ogoturuk, the Chukchi doesn't seem so terrifying anymore.

We get Blue settled in the kitchen with lots of food and water; then carry our packs down to the beach and load them into the rubber Zodiac. We dig up the anchor and wade out with the boat into the surf. Mike counts the waves. At his signal, Phoebe and Strider and I jump in (I do better this time). Strider kneels at the front and paddles hard; Mike jumps in just as the water is about to rise above his boots. He yanks several times at the starter cord before the motor engages, with Strider paddling and cursing all the time.

Then suddenly we're bouncing over the tops of the waves in a curtain of noise, cold, and spray. I'm holding on for dear life to the scalloped rope handles, just letting go briefly with one gloved hand to pull my cap down over my ears and tighten the hood of my cagoule. I'm positive that Mike is driving faster than he needs to, showing off: as we climb each hump of the swell we slap down violently on the other side; we thump rather than glide along with a motion that pulls at my breasts and hurts like horseback riding.

The birdwatchers strain forward for their first look at the colonies. Phoebe, her face full of color and drama when she turns once in a while to smile at me, is as zealous-looking as a missionary about to land on an island populated by cannibals.

I watch the strange chameleon coastline, as unreal as the different sets in a Hollywood movie studio—all front and no substance. We pass a stretch that looks like Utah, the cliff faces rising up in weird red-brown pinnacles; and then suddenly the land softens to rounded bluffs, covered with thick grass and wildflowers, and it's as if we're looking at the coast of Ireland. Then the bluffs give way to a moonscape as black and shiny as obsidian, etched by water dripping down from the tundra.

Clouds are building up again in the northwest, and my hands feel stiff in their deathgrip around the rope handles. Phoebe turns around and smiles, and I smile back at her, even though I'm feeling seasick and cold. Then Mike cuts in toward the shoreline and slows down. We drift under the shadow of a looming, striated cliff, slate-gray, black-and-white. As we come closer, I realize that the slate-gray part is the cliff, and the black-and-white is made of the birds that are nesting there.

Like a huge, vertical housing project, the cliff is a veritable slum of birds, one narrow ledgeful atop the other. I hear the birds chortling, and catch a whiff of their smell: fish and salt and sea grasses and guano.

"Those are murres," says Phoebe (the word rhymes with "hers"). "Thick-billed and commons. There're some kittiwakes, too, up higher on the cliff—can you see them? They're the small white gulls."

She hands me a pair of binoculars out of one of the packs; through them, I see a patch of the murres at close range, throwing their heads back and flapping their wings, diving off the cliffs into the water, pecking and fighting with each other, pointing their heads down to fuss with a single, aqua-colored egg under some of them, laid directly on the rock with no nesting materials at all. The birds are bullet-shaped, like penguins, with the same black-and-white tuxedo coloration; smooth, innocent black heads and throats; tiny black eyes, snow-white breasts, short black wings, and charcoal feet.

I lower the binoculars and am faced again with the unindividuated mass of black-and-white birds on the cliff. They all seem to be crying and chortling at once, shifting places on the rock ledge, falling off into the air, plopping down onto the water and diving under.

"We'll be counting these from the water," says Phoebe, "later on, during the census."

"Counting them?" I echo. "But they don't stand still."

"Neither will we while we're counting," says Mike. "We'll be moving up and down, and up and down," he says, moving up and down the scale with his voice.

"In that case, I'll be lying on the bottom of the boat," I say, "puking my guts out."

Strider removes his glasses, licks off the salt, and wipes the lenses carefully with a clean red bandana. "Not in my boat, you won't be."

"No sense in getting worked up over who's going to be puking in August when it's only July," says Phoebe. "Let's get going, big guy. Tay and I want to be in place for the one o'clock count."

Mike speeds up the motor and we turn north again, bouncing over the waves.

I am thoroughly queasy by the time we nose the boat in at the horseshoe-shaped beach that Phoebe identifies for me as Colony IV. She and I don packs and step out of the boat into the surf. Phoebe throws the wet bowline to Strider— the drops of water glint off it in the bright, cold air—and turns the boat around. We stand knee-deep in the surf and wave at Mike and Strider as they head further up the coast to collect murres for dissection and count the birds at Colony V, where they'll camp overnight.

The beach is coarse sand instead of shingle. A smaller creek than Ogoturuk runs into the Chukchi out of lush green hills. At their base, we take off our packs momentarily to change into our sneakers.

"There are two counting sites, up top," says Phoebe.

We're looking up the side of a steep cliff covered with green grass and wildflowers. The grass makes it look like it might not be too difficult to climb—but it will definitely be a climb, not a walk, uphill.

"All set?" she asks me. "Your color looks a little better now. Are you going to be able to manage the pack?"

I shift the pack slightly, testing its weight. I nod.

"You know," says Phoebe, "you remind me of my younger sister—she's a ballet dancer in New York." As she speaks, she adjusts my shoulder straps, tightening them. "My other sister—the eldest—is a model. A real-live international one—you'd probably recognize her face. She's so obsessed with what she does and doesn't eat, and with lifting weights and exercising, that she's just awful to be with! I visited her in Paris last year, and she wouldn't even go out to eat. In Paris! I could've killed her."

I wish we could just stand here and talk, but Phoebe gives a last tug on my pack and begins climbing. It seems an ominous note on which to leave our conversation. I follow behind her, climbing as fast as I can.

The hillside is wet and spongy and steep enough so that we have to climb hand over hand. Clumps of grass and dry roots come loose as I grab at them, filling my nose with the smell of growth and wet earth. Phoebe climbs with the surefootedness of a mountain goat, in long steady strides, without pausing. I have a final glimpse of her in silhouette far above me; and then find myself alone, clinging to the grass-covered cliff.

The weight of the pack, and the effort of balancing myself and it, has me sweating and out of breath. I'm unable to take more than one heavy slow step at a time, pausing to test my next wet foothold. When Phoebe disappears above me, I feel cut loose from all safety—as insubstantial as a puff of down that might suddenly blow off the side of the hill.

I turn around and look out toward the water to see if Mike and Strider are still there—but there is nothing but steel-gray emptiness, skimmed by the silhouettes of birds. Straight down I can still make out the two sets of boots, their tops folded down in case of rain.

Working as a secretary has, without question, been dull and numbing; but it has filled my hours and days and months and years with the certainty of other people's demands, leaving me bored and resentful but freed of the task of figuring out what I might want to do on my own. I've always been efficient at second-guessing other people's needs and fulfilling them, and I've hated myself when I've failed. I've listened so hard to that imagined harmony line that I've forgotten the trick of calling the main tune—of knowing what I want myself. And suddenly that knowledge is boiled down to something purely physical: I want to get to the top of these hills, to get to a place where I can set down my feet side by side and not have to cling with my hands. I want to remove this burden from my back and dry out my sweaty clothes. I want to not be alone any more on the side of this mountain like a cast-off feather, with nothing but empty space between me and the Chukchi Sea. There is nothing else that I want just now—nothing else seems to matter. The demand of the immediate has complete power over me: every inch of my animal being longs to be on level ground.

I try to imagine a rope between me and Phoebe, the kind that mountain climbers use. We *are* tied together, the two of us. We were literally tied together as we pulled in the whale. We are tied together, not with a rope but by experience, because of Mike. Suddenly even that connection is reassuring, one more knot uniting us. I would *be* Phoebe if I were more heroic. As it is, I am her shadow, tied to her by a lifeline; her child, tied to her by an umbilical cord. I do feel infinitely small and embryonic, stretched in both directions, down and up: down toward the suicidal hole of our boots at the base of the hill, up toward Phoebe and unknown light. And in the middle of this tug-of-war, I hear Phoebe's voice calling down to me, "Tay!"

It is finally like being pulled up to the top: I land in a plentitude of blue flowers and green grass that feels as deeply layered as mattresses piled one atop the other. Cold sunlight pours down, peeling off the softening blur of distances so that everything seems to stand out in crystalline detail, as if seen through a magnifying lens. I see individual blades of grass far across the cliff-top meadow. Phoebe has let down the hood of her parka, and I see her hair blowing back from her fine-grained skin. I lope toward her, hearing the scrape of the legs of my jeans, one against the other; the weight of my pack no longer bothers me. No more strings pull me downward: I'm cut loose from everything down below. We are both, gloriously, at the top.

Phoebe claps me on the shoulder, and we walk on together across the meadow and scramble up over some rocks. At the very crest of the hill, where the wind blows hardest, we drop our packs and build the tent—the same stained-glass blue one that I slept in alone when we first arrived.

The Chukchi spreads out below us like a silver mirror. Checking her watch, Phoebe leads us down to the other edge of the cliff for the one o'clock count.

* * *

A twenty-four hour count is one piece in a puzzle that, when assembled, provides scientists with a picture of an avian population. Birds don't have the courtesy to stand still during the two or three days it may take to count a population along the coast; so an attempt is made to correct for variations in their numbers by counting one group over and over again at evenly spaced times during the day and night. Plots are marked out on a map, and subgroups of the colony are counted every two hours through twenty-four-hour periods once a week. Since it takes an hour to get to the upper colonies by boat from the field-camp, the census-takers must camp out at the counting site.

Colony IV is perched atop a cliff towering five hundred feet above a horseshoe-shaped beach. The site is divided into two parts facing each other on opposite ends of the horseshoe, with some two hundred birds variably occupying the imagined significant grids in between. The place we sit for counting at site A is on two flat rocks amidst meadow grass that drops off suddenly into air. Site B is higher up on bare rock overhanging the sea. We must walk carefully, because the rock is decomposing from the guano that falls day after day, night after night.

At site A there is a glaucous gull nesting in the tall grass. She dive-bombs us as we pick our steps through the grass to the flat rock, swooping past our ears and turning to hover in the air facing us, her gullet throbbing with a threatened barrage of regurgitated fish. Even though it is the same two people every time, and we walk quietly and harm nothing, the glaucous gull keeps up her attack with the same intensity every hour, like an earnest actress rehearsing a part again and again. She barks in our ears with the noise of an infuriated Chihuahua.

We look through binoculars at the opposite cliff, trying to separate out individual birds from the mass of black and white, giving one click of the thumb for each bird on a mechanical counter that keeps a tally of the total. I find it difficult to coordinate this process of seeing and clicking, especially when the objects being counted are in constant motion, jostling each other with their bills and wings, leaping up into the air like angels, swooping off toward the water like teacups falling off a shelf.

Phoebe and I count in tandem at the beginning—I suppose because my first tallies are bound to be unreliable. The wind is cold and wet in our faces, and our hands are stiff and clumsy in wet wool gloves. The warm breath of our eyes fogs the lenses of the binoculars; our hair escapes from our hoods into our mouths. The glaucous gull makes another visitation like a wicked witch, her black eyes gleaming and glazed, flying insanely against the head-wind as she hangs suspended in one place.

Dearest Peg and Denny,

What is it like on the arctic coast at nine P.M. in the summer? The rain falls noiselessly into the lush green grass that grows on the cliff-tops as thick as the fur of an animal, feeling equally alive underfoot. Imagine a flower garden with all the flowers shrunk to the size of peas and grains of rice: they are still recognizable to the eye that can expand them (the artist who made the world has no sense of scale). Even with no eye to see them, the forget-me-nots bloom in thick blue carpets; the anemones are as bright as broken-up suns. Imagine a willow tree that for thirty years has had only three months a year for growing, and must spend one of these months simply growing warm. Imagine a grove of willows twisting gnarled trunks at the height of your shins. Their branches bend backwards into the grass with the weight of outsized red blossoms. Imagine a willow so cold and so small that it grows as lichen.

I am awake suddenly, but I don't open my eyes. I'm much warmer than I was when I fell asleep. A body radiating heat is plastered against my back, its knees curled up under my knees, as close as my own shadow.

Phoebe—the magnificent, the sublime—forgot the sleeping bags. With many apologies, she let me rest after we'd finished the first five counts together. I wrote a note to Peg and Denny, then put my extra socks over my hands and curled up on the floor of the tent, but I couldn't get warm.

After staring so long at them, I couldn't help thinking of the murres out there on the edge of the cliff, exposed to the arctic wind. The noise of the colony was reduced to a distant purr from inside the tent. Occasionally an insomniac bird let out a lone aggressive cry, or a bird passed directly overhead, the wind whistling past its wings with a sound like a flute being breathed over but not quite played—a kind of protomusic. I lay there thinking of the people in Berkeley who sleep on the sidewalk all winter long, people who are there because something went wrong—either in their brains or in the hearts and minds of people around them: people who are mad or drunk or wishing they were drunk; people needing a fix, people needing a psychiatrist; but most of all, people needing warmth: a sleeping bag, a blanket, a shelter. I am used to walking by them—in some cases, walking over them—with guilt and disgust and pity. I have given quarters, I have looked away: but never once have I offered something warm. I've walked away hugging my warmth to myself, or, more usually on such streets on such nights, hugging the warm or indifferent arm of my companion. With such thoughts I must have fallen, finally, into a frigid sleep.

I do not open my eyes now because I know that the shadow is Phoebe, that the arm slung over my hip is hers, that the radiating warmth beneath my bottom is coming from her body, pressed up against mine.

The warmth is nice. Phoebe is snoring lightly. If I push her, however gently, away, I will be cold again. If I don't stir and simply fall back to sleep, she'll never have to know that I have agreed in any way to this embrace. And perhaps it's accidental, anyway. I have always, in my desire to confirm my presence in the world, imagined that people are lusting after me. Often it has turned out to be idle, wishful thinking: a terrible, distorting desire to be loved.

I've caught myself, during my walks across campus to work, imagining that each person I passed was thinking of me, that they actually cared about the way I looked, registered what I was wearing and how I had put it all together—judged me, in short, as I judged them. I've had to check myself with the reminder that I'm an object of indifference to these students hurrying off to their classes: a paper-pusher, someone who has no worth as an individual, whose imagination doesn't count; a factotum of the university.

In her sleep, Phoebe probably mistook me for Mike: and the arm and the warmth and the close fit of the shadow are not meant for me at all. Maybe when she wakes up, she'll think that I have engineered myself into this position of intimacy, stealing the warmth meant for her husband. She will never look at me the same way after that; she'll believe that I've revealed myself as a lesbian.

Could it be true? Do I feel any stirrings where Phoebe's

thighs are pressed up against me so vividly even through all our layers of clothes? Perhaps it's true—perhaps I've been a lesbian all this time without somehow knowing about it, and that's why I lived with Morgie for three years, who turned out, after all, to prefer men; and why I've never managed to get married, and still don't have children. Is it possible to discover that you're someone quite different from the person you had always imagined yourself to be after twenty-nine years? It happened to Morgie, after all! I hold my breath, trying to feel my feelings; trying to find a moment of perfect honesty.

I don't know what it feels like to feel like a lesbian—how will I know? I feel warmth, coziness. I adore Phoebe—I really do. But I don't feel the need for anything more. Warmth and love: we lie here entwined and the moment is quite complete; the moment is already consummated. I don't have a name for this thing between us, surrounding us like a halo.

Phoebe is leaning over me, gently pressing two fingers against my forehead. I remember this from yoga classes, a gentle way to awaken someone: she is opening my third eye. "Tay. It's your turn now," she says. Her voice makes breath-clouds in the dim, blue-tinted air of the tent.

"Hi," I mumble. "What time is it?"

"A quarter to four. Put your shoes on and eat some chocolate. Go pee if you have to and count the birds at site *A*. Count them *twice*, Tay! Then do the same thing at *B*. Then curl up and rest somewhere, but don't fall asleep. I'll be up to help you for the seven o'clock count. Here's my watch—I don't know why Mike didn't buy you one of your own."

It is reassuring just now to hear a string of orders, even though my body resists being pulled out of warmth and sleep. As I piss outside, steam rises up from the cold ground. I feel like a great animal—some crude brown mare—standing out in a field. I break off a quarter of the bittersweet chocolate bar and stuff it in my jacket pocket along with the counter and Phoebe's yellow field notebook. The glow of warmth is already leaving me; the binoculars feel as heavy as a harness around my neck.

The colony is quieter, the light brighter, than when I last counted. I sit carefully on the flat rock, missing something; then I realize that the glaucous gull has finally not come out from its nest to scold and threaten. The wind is still blowing cold and steady into my face. As I sit counting, alone, I feel like a sailor far out at sea.

When I finish at the two sites, I turn my back to the Chukchi and the wind, trying to pick out a sheltered spot among the sandstone cliffs and grass-covered bluffs. I find a dimple in the rocks, a sort of half-cave, that seems just suited for a body to curl up in. Lichen grows over it like green velvet.

So stupid, really, my agonies of the morning: Phoebe was just being human and companionable under the circumstances. She was being simple and appropriate while I was caught up in my own convolutions. Here, in the carved-out shelter of the earth itself, in my own primordial cave, I have a sudden larger sense of things. My revelation is almost too simple not to sound simple-minded. It's simply the larger sense of being part of things: of the birds on the cliff, of the people on the street, of Phoebe's warmth and friendship, of the very landscape itself.

Nine

~~~~~~~~~

At six A.M., I'm sitting on the upper cliff at site *B*, counting the birds, when a fog suddenly blows in from the sea. I wait, huddled in my jacket, for another gust of wind to clear it away, but the fog remains, making it impossible to see across to the other side.

It's no use to sit here freezing if I can't count, so I gather myself up and cross back down the bluff, pausing at a trickle of water to drink. As I kneel, a tiny gold and yellow animal crawls out from a hole in the uneven ground and chatters at me, cocking its head first to one side and then to the other. I stay perfectly still, holding my breath. The creature—no bigger than my outstretched hand—stalks up to me, touches my bent knee with its tiny forepaw, turns a sommersault, runs in two clockwise circles, stands up and chatters, then slips back into the hole as if sucked inside by a vacuum.

I wait without moving for this tiny vision to reappear, but finally my foot falls asleep and I give up, limping through the white mist to the tent. Leaving my shoes outside, I unzip the flap and lay down near Phoebe, hugging her close against me.

"Fog roll in?" she asks without moving.

I continue to lie close, but relax my hold, suddenly self-conscious about my hands. "How could you tell?"

"The birds got quiet all of a sudden and the wind stopped. I heard you coming back early, and figured there was fog." She pauses. "I guess we might as well both get some sleep." We lie quietly, our breath even, but not the deeper breathing of sleep.

Phoebe speaks again just as I'm drifting off. "I lied about it being me that wanted you to come along. It was Mike that wanted you."

I take a long time to answer. "I sort of guessed that, Phoebe. But it doesn't matter. It's nothing serious."

Phoebe snorts. "Oh, it's never anything serious with Mike."

"You mean—you mean he does this often?"

"Well, you didn't think you were the first, did you?"

How strange it is to be lying here, holding Phoebe, and having this conversation. "I didn't think about it, at the time. I mean, I assumed he wasn't married. I was very attracted to him—strictly in a physical sort of way." A long pause. "I didn't know you knew."

Phoebe answers right away. "I didn't."

There is noise outside of the colony awakening. The sky lightens, turning the air in the tent pale blue flecked with gold. I don't say anything. What *can* I say?

"Oh, I figured as much—don't feel that you've just given yourself away. I'd rather have everything out in the open, anyway." She's quiet for a moment. "He's always been like that, since the beginning, when it was *my* shorts he was trying to get into."

I prop myself up on one elbow so that I might see Phoebe's expression, but she remains turned away from me. I plunk back down and ask quietly, "Why do you put up with him?"

"Oh, Mike and I go back a long way. You do things when you're younger that you'd never even consider doing later on. But I like to stick to a decision once I've made it."

This reasoning seems very wrong to me—and not at all an adequate explanation for putting up with constant repetitions of betrayal: it must, it *must* hurt Phoebe. But I can't say any of this to her—I don't know her well enough. "How did you two meet?" I ask instead.

Phoebe sighs. "My older sister—the model—went to college with Mike, out in Colorado. He was madly in love with her, just like everyone else was. It was in the summer just after I finished high school—you know, the Summer of Love. Mike blew into town on the biggest motorcycle we'd ever seen. It was one of those Harley-Davidsons that the Hell's Angels ride and it made as much noise as a machine gun. We lived in a small town, and things like that made a big impression on people. Anyway, Adelaide—my sister—was away in New York when Mike came looking for her. He didn't come with any more information than the name of the town. But my uncle, my father's brother, owns a gift shop on the main street, and Mike recognized the name and came in asking about Adelaide.

"I was working in the shop for the summer, saving up money for college. Mike was pretty disappointed, I guess, but he put on a good show and gave me a ride on his motorcycle, and I invited him home to dinner, and my mother got out the family album and he got to see all these pictures of Adelaide as a little girl, Adelaide in the bathtub, Adelaide dressed up for Halloween. Of course, being as far gone over her as he was, he ate it up; and my mother just went crazy—no one outside the family had ever been so enthusiastic about her album before. She even got out this ancient movie projector and showed home movies of Adelaide's birthday parties against the dining-room wall.

"By the time Mike left, my mother thought he was just about the most wonderful young man in the world—which surprised me, since she always said she hated motorcycles. I guess it was those blue eyes that won her over.

"A couple of years later—after Adelaide was already pretty famous—Mike showed up at my college. Not as a student or anything; he was just visiting. I thought it was weird, since I knew how he felt about Adelaide; but he acted just like he'd forgotten her. He hung around for a couple of weeks, taking me out to dinner and sending me flowers and stuff. All my friends were really impressed— you know, this older man. Then about six months later, I got a letter from him saying that he was going to go to graduate school in Alaska, and he wondered if I would like to go with him. He didn't exactly say anything about marriage, but once my mother got wind of it, one thing led to another.

"I really thought Mike was pretty romantic, and I couldn't see trying to do what either one of my sisters was doing—I wasn't gorgeous like Adelaide, and I wasn't built to be a dancer like Penny. Alaska sounded just fine—like a big fine adventure. We'd be like nineteenth-century pioneers. I had just declared myself an anthropology major, and I thought—whoopee—just think of all those old bones up there. Are you awake?"

" 'Think of all those old bones up there,' " I murmur. "Had he really gotten over Adelaide?"

"I used to wonder about that a lot. Then I decided that it wasn't really Adelaide he'd been in love with—it was more like some kind of idea of—I don't know. Of glamour. Of something you know you can't have, but you go on wanting it anyway. Adelaide has visited us a couple of times, and we see her about every other Christmas; and Mike says he thinks she's too self-involved, and sort of cadaverous-looking. She looked better, in person at least, when she was in college. These models lead a pretty unhealthy life."

"Were you in love with Mike?"

There's a long pause, then Phoebe turns over on her back and yawns. I can see that she's been crying—somehow, noiselessly. The tears have left little snail's tracks down her cheeks. "I don't know. He's been more like a brother, in a way. I always wished I had a brother, especially after my dad died. Mike was so different from any of us. He just did whatever made him happy, and he liked making other people happy, too. He didn't get neurotic about things the way a lot of people do. You know, we girls were always thinking, 'Should I do this? Should I do that? How will that affect everyone else?' All that sort of thing. Mike seemed so much more natural, somehow. He's one of the few people I've ever known who had a really happy childhood—right out of a storybook. He grew up on a farm."

And took his morality from the barnyard, I guess. I would like to say this, but restrain myself. Of course, there are two sides to every story, and I haven't really heard Mike's version yet—not that I have any expectation that I ever will. I try to imagine what it *would* be like to be married to someone like Phoebe—I mean, to someone who was really, heroically, strong. It's what every woman wants (or thinks she wants)—but how would it be for a man?

We lie there in silence, listening to the day breaking all over the colony as more and more birds join in the chorus of complaints and cries, ready to start the cycle once more of feeding and washing and focusing all their warmth down onto those eggs. "Mike told me years later," says Phoebe, "that his college advisor had told him not to go up to Alaska without a woman—there were even fewer women up here in those days, before the pipeline. So he just thought about it and then decided on me. It was sort of a political decision—like arranged marriages in the old days, except Mike was doing his own arranging. I guess he saw that I was easy-going. It's worked out pretty well. A lot of girls I knew in college are divorced now, or on a second or even a third marriage. You ever been married?"

"No. I was living with a man I hoped to marry—but he decided he was a homosexual."

"Jesus!" says Phoebe. "What a bummer!"

"Yeah. That's exactly what it was." A light rain begins to fall. I really don't feel like talking about Morgie. All of a sudden, I feel really sick of the subject of marriage and men; sick at heart. I get up on my knees and reach for the zipper of the tent flap. "It must be a sun shower," I tell Phoebe; but she stops my hand before I can get the flap open.

"Guess again, city girl!" She runs an ungloved forefinger over the window netting. In the greenish light, I see the needlelike tails of insects thrust through the tiny holes, and can vaguely make out the blurred whirring of their wings.

"Mosquitoes," says Phoebe. "They can smell our blood." She plucks off one intruding proboscis, then another, just like slipping a honeysuckle flower off its stem.

"Does that kill them?"

Phoebe goes on plucking. "Eventually. It makes it so they can't feed any more and they starve to death."

"That's kind of sadistic, isn't it?"

Phoebe tucks in her shirt and looks at her watch. "We'll just be able to make the seven o'clock count. You tell me in an hour about how sadistic it is."

I reach for the zipper again. "Let me go first," she says. She unzips the flap, slips deftly out, and zips it back down again. A tiny swarm has managed to come in anyway and buzzes close to my eyes. Phoebe puts on her shoes, then slips mine inside, along with a small white plastic bottle of bug repellant. "Put this on all your exposed skin. It'll at least keep them from biting."

All coated with bug dope, I emerge from the tent, my head filled with images from Phoebe's story. I start to say something, but my mouth fills with insects. I spit, then try to wipe them out with my fingers, spreading the taste of poison inside my mouth. My shirtsleeves are covered with a fine red net of mosquitoes. They hover close to the moist surface of my eyes and nostrils and mouth, seek out the labyrinth of my ears, touch the skin of my face and wrists with a thousand hairlike legs.

Phoebe leads and I follow her, squinting against the swarm of bugs. The mosquitoes are waiting for a chance to enter my flesh; the bug dope provides only the thinnest impediment. I try to imagine being up in the air in a plane, far above the wet meadow grass and the bluff, staring down at the two lone mammals in a landscape of plants.

"Whose blood do they suck when we're not here?" I ask Phoebe through clenched teeth. I am unable to keep from waving my hands in front of my face and over my head, brushing away palpable clouds of tiny bodies and wings.

"They usually live on green things," answers Phoebe, her arms hanging composedly by her sides (Mike is not the only one, apparently, who feels compelled to show off). The reddish bugs look like an aureole around her head painted by a *pointilliste*. "It's only in breeding season that they need blood for extra strength, so that they can lay their eggs. They bite whatever's available. Inland they're so bad that whole herds of caribou will stampede in a frenzy down to the coast to try to get in a breeze."

It's the first day since we arrived at Darwin that the air is still, as if the fog had somehow stolen away with it the atmosphere's ability to breathe. I can hear my own breaths coming in tiny repressed puffs. I can feel something building up in me that must be what the caribou feel: a sense of panic. It's only through an intense effort of will and a tension that makes my arms twitch that I'm able to keep myself from breaking into an hysterical scream. The high-pitched buzzing of the insects so overwhelms my ears that it spills over fantastically into the other senses, seeming almost to have a smell, like electricity gone wrong somehow, the smell that an epileptic senses before having a seizure.

The bugs thin out a little in the breeze on the edge of the cliff where we pick our way carefully down to the counting site. Now I know why Phoebe pitched our tent on the unsheltered crest of the hill. Through binoculars, I can see that the murres are also twitching under attacking hoards of bugs. I do not just feel empathy for them now—I feel *of* them, as if the world were simplemindedly divided into two camps: the insects and everyone else. The murres and Phoebe and I are in the same camp together, miserably besieged.

We finish at the first site, and are in the middle of counting the second when the wind comes up suddenly, as if the stillness had only been a breath held in by someone diving deep underwater, and now the diver surfaces and lets his breath out in a great panting gasp. The mosquitoes scatter.

I toss my head around, searching for the remnants of my sanity. The burning smell is gone. The birds stand in a tranquil pose that looks like an expression of gratitude. Then, almost as one, they turn their bodies in toward the cliff, the brooding birds pressing close against their single, pear-shaped eggs, their backs to the sea.

Phoebe nudges me and points downward over the water. Not far away is the bobbing Zodiac, with Mike and Strider inside. Through our binoculars we can see them gesturing an urgent demand for us to come down. Beyond them, on the horizon, a rain squall seems to be eating up the sky in a mass of poisonous yellow-brown, moving toward us. The Chukchi is whipped up in a fury of whitecaps.

Phoebe says, "Oh, Jesus!", then grabs my hand. "Come on, Tay. Hurry!" It's the first time I've ever heard her sound afraid.

Whereas before we stepped gingerly over the crumbling rocks, we now run back up the hill to where our tent is pitched, empty it out, and pull up our stakes. Phoebe barks orders while I help her roll the tent up into its bag. I stand as passive as a mule while Phoebe loads a pack, our tent, and our cookstove onto my back. Somehow, we seem to have ended up with much more than we had when we climbed the hill—or perhaps it's just not packed as carefully: but Phoebe winds up with an even larger and more cumbersome load on her back. It's impossible to run, or even to walk quickly; and yet Phoebe is soon far ahead of me, outlined against the horizon like an old-world pedlar, dwarfed under her huge shapeless load. I am panting to catch up with her, and terrified that I am going to lose my balance and roll down the mountain like a loose boulder.

In the last hand-over-hand climb, I slide more than walk, scraping away fistfuls of mud and grass, grabbing at the tiny willow branches, dislodging patches of blue flowers. In our descent, it has grown as dark as nighttime, with lightning gashes across the sky. Rain pelts down first as sheets, then as hail. We drop our packs at the bottom of the slope and pull on our hip-boots, running the final fifty yards across the beach to the sea.

The boat, which is out beyond the breakers, seems to be getting further away rather than coming in. Strider is frantically bailing water. Phoebe wades into the surf up to her knees and I follow her, a new sense of panic spreading across my chest. Mike shouts at us through cupped hands, but his words are drowned in the storm. Finally I make out the words, but I can't believe that he's saying them: "We can't land! You've got to swim!"

I start laughing. No one can swim in the Chukchi—even I know that. Phoebe suddenly turns toward me, her face very close to mine. She's about to kiss me. This makes me laugh even harder, so that my sides start to ache. But the only thing to land on me is a slap on the jaw.

"Don't go flaky on me now, Tay!" she's shouting at me. "This storm may last for weeks and the boat's leaving with or without us." Working quickly, she pulls off her boots in the knee-deep water, and throws them one at a time toward the foundering boat. Mike catches one, and the other lands in the water, but Strider fishes it out with the dip-net used for retrieving birds that have been shot on the wing out at sea. Phoebe shouts into my face, "Take off your boots and swim!"; and then flings herself into the water and strikes out for the boat.

Then time slows down, because there is so little of it left. It's as if I'm watching a movie on TV all about Mike and Strider pulling Phoebe into a boat that seems to be riding dangerously low on the water. Then the movie's over and it's time for bed. I pull off my beautiful black leather boots—the ones I bought in Spain—and toss them into the closet; and this is very strange, because I am always careful about placing their cardboard stiffeners inside and setting each boot upright on the carpeted floor. That's why they've lasted all these years. I'm so tired! I feel like I'm just going to die if I don't lie down immediately. I dive into the rumpled flannel sheets, my lovely flannel sheets, and bury my head in my favorite down pillow. And suddenly I'm in the middle of a nightmare which has the same setting as the movie I've just been watching about Phoebe, only a thousand tiny razor blades are slicing my skin, and I am trying to move my arms, but my brain is dying, and the razor blades have changed to warm tongues, and in some part of myself I know that this is even worse. I turn and sleep and then dream again that I am a fish that has been caught; and as I rise into the air I am suffocating because I can no longer breathe, and the whole world is only the flash of my silver scales, so bright that they reflect across the sky.

Then I wake up again, lying on top of something soft and cold. I shift my weight and look down and see that the dream has changed again, and I am lying in the bottom of a boat on top of a row of dead murres attached to each other by a cord tied above their pale charcoal webbed feet. Their eyes are frozen in various attitudes of panic. They give off the smell of fish and death and blood.

Phoebe lies beside me breathing heavily and shivering. Her face is a strange color that looks like the pure white breast-feathers of the dead birds. I am worried that Phoebe might die, too, and try to lift my arm so that I can put it around her. But there's no feeling at all in my arm, and I've lost the trick for moving it. The same is true for my legs, so that when the vomit rises up with the sting of salt in my throat, there is nothing I can do but retch helplessly near my own head. When I start to choke, Mike comes up from behind me and holds me by my hair as I hang as limp as a rag doll over the side. There isn't much inside me but seawater and chocolate to vomit up. Occasionally Mike reaches back to drive the boat while Strider bails out the blood-stained water. The motor shorts and a shock runs through Mike to me, and I feel it at the tips of my fingers and in the center of my brain. Maybe this is a new way of talking, without words, without sound: just a direct jolt to the brain. We would never tell lies if we talked this way. We would never prevaricate. We would be connected as the whales are connected in the depths of the sea.

Ten

I am lying on a hard bed. The sound of the arctic wind roars in my ears, even here in the hospital room: I can hear the plastic windows collapsing and inflating again as they're buffeted by the wind. Or is it the sound of my own heart pumping, my lungs collapsing and inflating again?

There's not enough air in this room. It's overheated; there's no privacy. Doctors are performing operations behind my back. They're dissecting cadavers. They hold each part up in the air, weigh it, write down its weight, then toss it onto a heap smelling of dried blood and feathers. When I breathe, I can hear the rattle of water in my lungs. I am sweating, but no one has come for days to bathe me. I try to call out for a nurse, but I can't get enough air. Finally, I'm screaming, and I sit bolt upright, awake.

One of the doctors walks up to me and puts his hand on my forehead. He isn't wearing the right clothes, and his hand stinks of death and the sea. He's young, with liquid brown eyes. In a nice voice that reminds me of my cousins from Chicago, he remarks that my fever seems to be going down. Then I hear Strider's voice saying, "Come on, Mosher, these gonads are all going to putrify before we can measure them." The young man with the nice voice and smelly hands gives me a look of apology and turns back to the kitchen table, which is littered with dead, split-open murres and a pile of their offal in a dish of blood-stained cornmeal. I feel like I'm going to vomit, and then suddenly I do, although it's nothing but dry-heaving; I am completely empty. I put my hand up to my damp hair, and for a tiny moment I care about how awful I must look; then I don't care anymore. I sit up, my legs tangled in the heavy sleeping bag. "Where's Phoebe?" I ask, and my voice rings out clear and new.

"Welcome back from the dead," says Mike from the table, dangling a dead murre by one black foot. "We moved Phoebe into the sleeping-shed because she was complaining about the heat. She said to give you her love when you woke up."

He says it facetiously, but I can hear Phoebe's message anyway—it's real, and it means a great deal to me. Mike can't even speak of love, least of all the love between two friends, without belittling it somehow. I have a sudden image of creatures bigger and more powerful than ourselves measuring the balls of these men, these heroes. They're all afraid, these great big swaggering men; quaking in their boots, peeing in their pants. The whole culture is built up to obscure this one essential fact: the men are also weak, the men are afraid. We help in the construction; we lay down our very bodies as bricks in the wall, turning our faces away from the secret inside. But we still want heroes—not reflections of our own doubt. The whole assemblage is a fiction, but everyone works together to uphold it, and we don't tell the men that we know, or even each other. Because if we did, the wall would collapse, and the men would be standing naked together in the place of concealment, forever exposed as frauds; and we would be left with only our own aspirations, wild and terrifying, filled with the possibility of failure, our very strength oppressive and embarrassing and nearly uncontainable, still looking for a man to house the illusion, to make it more seemly. And I understand, taste it like ashes in my mouth, that even in the midst of my realization I touched my hand to my hair and regretted that I couldn't look beautiful for the young man, the new man with the liquid brown eyes.

I wake up again. The birds have been pushed off to one side of the table. I smell meat and onions frying. Phoebe is standing in front of the stove, stirring a pot of beans and giving instructions to the young man, Robbie, and to Strider, who is cutting up breast meat from the murres. I can see vegetables, fruit, and eggs: Bill did make it in after all, and he must have brought Robbie with him. I have to clear my throat for a long time before the words will come out. "My letters," I croak. "I wanted to send them back out with Bill."

"Bill thought of it himself," says Mike. "He had me look in your room—I found three big fat ones."

Phoebe walks over and gives me a kiss, first on the forehead and then on the mouth, just as if no one else were there. "God, I was afraid you were going to die! They said you swam like a fish and didn't pass out until you were a couple of feet from the boat."

I smile up at her. I can't remember the last time a woman kissed me on the lips—maybe Peg did, but it was ages ago. It's like an exchange of secret knowledge, given and taken without words. Phoebe will go on loving Mike, struggling to make something good out of their marriage, to look away while he does his romance and big-blue-eyes bit with strangers, the slow, loving orgasms bestowed like long-stemmed roses; and brings Phoebe home his dirty underwear, and loves her selfishly and comes too quickly, and keeps her at arm's length like a madonna, and hates her for disillusioning him constantly while he's trying to worship her—as she's unveiled, bit by bit, and he learns of her sweat and smelly feet and her farts and her shit and her breath in the morning and the little black hairs around her nipples and the stink of her crotch, and all her awful humanity. And I'll go on looking for a hero, because it's too terrifying to contemplate being a hero myself, or to admit that if I try to be successful, to commit myself to something, I run the risk of failure. But the balloon has a hole in it now, and the patch is just a shuck. But somehow the charade is all right; and I feel reassured by Phoebe's kiss. We'll go on play-acting, because we're stronger than the men: it was Phoebe and I who swam in the Chukchi and lived to tell.

"Murre tacos," says Robbie. "How does that sound to you?"

I look up feeling completely naked. I taste my stale breath as I answer him. "I think I'd like a pot of water and a sponge."

"The creek's gone completely muddy," says Phoebe. "We don't even have enough drinking water—just what's here." She points to the plastic bucket with a cover on it and kicks a five-gallon can filled with rusty-looking water.

"That's okay," I say, meaning it. I guess no one could have thought of Bill's handkerchief—all washed and folded as smoothly as I could manage without an iron. I meant to give it back to him when he landed; to keep my promise.

I walk over to the stove in my tee shirt and panties, pull my steaming bluejeans off the clothesline and step into them. No one seems to notice, and no one says anything. I feel that I've become something else—not a woman, not a girl: just one of the people. Grabbing a broom, I start sweeping up the feathers that litter the floor. The wind roars down the stovepipe with a wild, drunken sound, reminding me of the drunk who sang outside the Miner's Dream Motor Lodge after Mike and I made love.

I look over at Mike, over space and time: from this distance, our love-making looks small and perfect and contained, like a clear beautiful gem in a velvet box. It was in another era, a million years ago: a small, precious gift from the gods. For the first time ever, I smile at Mike as a friend. I can smile at him now and still love Phoebe with all my heart: both things can be held within me and contemplated at the same time. Perhaps I've grown physically larger to have so much room inside me.

We are stupid creatures, with short memories. We only remember how wonderful it is to breathe freely when we have colds, or the simple pleasure of drinking water when we have suffered thirst. Suffering just a little is a way of reaffirming all our pleasures—to be thirsty, to drink; to fast, to eat; to be lonely, to be loved. We don't know we are alive until we are hit over the head and feel the intensity of our pain.

Surviving the Chukchi has made me think about how I might *not* have survived. In a way, I don't feel that I lived so much as that I've changed: a different person was fished up out of those waters. I feel—more sensitive, somehow: as if all my nerve endings had spread out and enlarged over the surface of my skin. The sea poured through me, washed me out; left me parched but tantalizingly alive.

The storm had abated only once, just long enough for Bill to fly up with Robbie Mosher and our supplies; for me, it's been one continuous, unending storm. Since I've been better, I've bundled up and walked down to the beach every day to stare at the sea and pick up stones. In the kitchen, I take them out of my pockets and spread them out on the table. I wet them to bring out their colors: moss-green rocks striated with black, slate-gray stones spotted with amber— miniatures of the cliffs at the colonies.

Phoebe looks up from the notebook where she's record-ing measurements of the dead murre bodies. "Those look just like the pebbles I shook out of my boots this morning."

"Each one is so special," I say to her. "Look at this one—it looks like a tiny, primitive painting of an Eskimo. Do you see the fishing pole?" I hold up the stone for her to examine.

"Listen to her," says Mike. "Acid eyes."

"LSD," says Phoebe when I look over at her for an explanation. "We'd drop acid and then kind of get stuck looking at things. It didn't matter what; it all looked beautiful."

Acid. I was too young when all that was happening. Just a couple of years behind. I was a freshman in high school during the Summer of Love.

Suddenly I notice that everyone else is working while I'm contemplating my cache of rocks and my past. "Can I help?" I ask.

Phoebe smiles and pushes aside her notebook. "I'd like to take a break," she says.

Phoebe's job was weighing the birds, then recording all the measurements as they're made by the others. I take her place at the table. Touching death—even seeing it—makes my heart beat quickly, my stomach churn, and my mouth go dry. But my innate revulsion—or is it a conditioned revulsion?—can be pushed aside and overcome, it seems, with some effort of will.

Mike shows me how to attach each bird by one of its feet to a hand-held spring balance; and then I record the bird's weight next to its code number. Strider explains about examining the brood patch, a highly vascularized place at the breast that gradually becomes bald when the birds are incubating an egg. We rate the brood patch according to how nearly bald it is, from one to four. The threes and fours are the birds that have been successful in producing an egg this year; although, this late in the season, Strider tells me, probably only the fours will manage to fledge a chick on time, before the cold weather sets in. Robbie cuts through the snowy white feathers into the sternum; and cracks open the chest cavity. He takes out the stomach and covers it with formaldehyde in a neatly labelled glass jar. Mike measures the bird's subcutaneous fat and the size of its reproductive organs. Then the used-up corpse is added to a pile of dead and mutilated birds on the storm porch outside.

Some of the birds are twenty or twenty-five years old. By measuring them and seeing what they've been eating, we can supposedly gauge the success of the entire colony—or other scientists, using our data, will be able to do so later on. But I can't help asking myself if it's fair. Is the knowledge gained weighty enough to balance against the ending of life? The birds sit exposed on the cliff in all weather, warming the egg, then feeding the chick—their lives completely dedicated to reproduction. There are over two hundred fifty thousand birds in the colony. Does one life matter? Or four? Or twenty? For each dead bird with a naked brood patch there is a partner waiting on an egg, waiting mindlessly to be relieved of its duty so that it can fly off and wash and drink and feed. After a while, it will just as mindlessly give up, abandoning the egg or the chick to the hunger of a glaucous gull or a falcon or the wind.

As I touch the dead birds, holding their unresisting weight in my hands, I feel suddenly aware of my own soft skin, full of electricity. I feel afraid of being touched, afraid I might break into flames like dry wood. This morning I felt my ovulation: a tiny cramping on my left side. Afterwards, I lay in bed wondering if I might possibly be able to feel my cells dividing. I lay on my side listening to the rush of blood to my brain.

Mike announces that it's time for me to learn to use a shotgun. Since I get seasick, I will be making hourly counts alone on one of the beaches—another balancing measure—while the others count from the boats. Apparently, grizzly bears sometimes come down to the beach looking for food: if they see a person there, walled in by the towering cliffs, they might panic and charge. I cannot even vaguely imagine killing a bear, but Mike is insistent that I learn how. He picks up one of the two shotguns, wiping it off with an oily rag. Phoebe takes the gun away from him.

"I'll show her," she says.

Mike says, "Suit yourself, Feeble. You're a better shot than I am, anyway."

Phoebe and I walk out a little to the north of the camp near a rise of land that's fenced in with white-painted boards protecting a grave mound, topped by two more of the fence-boards nailed into a cross.

"Is this for inspiration?" I ask her.

She points to a rusty oil drum nearby, standing alone on the tundra. "That's our target," she says, holding the gun sideways and showing me how to open the magazine and load in the cartridges. "You pull down on the slide—here—to let a cartridge down into the chamber."

I look across the barrel of the gun at the grave mound. "Who's buried here?" I ask Phoebe.

"No one's too sure. One story is that a couple of army men overwintered here to make weather measurements; and one of them died of exposure. Another has it that it's an Eskimo's grave. That's the one I believe. The Eskimos are very big on Christianity."

The whole thing makes me uncomfortable—target practice in a cemetery. Phoebe places the gun in my arms, showing me how to support its weight and sight along the barrel.

"The top third of the oil drum, dead-center, is the bear's heart," she explains. "Bears have pretty thick skulls, so you don't want to try aiming at the head—you'd have to shoot it right through the eye. Aim for the heart."

I lower the gun. "Phoebe, how much chance is there that I'll really have to use this thing?"

"Very, very little. We haven't had anyone shooting directly at a bear during the ten years we've been coming out to Darwin. But you've got to know how, just on that odd chance."

The air is relatively warm, with a light breeze, but still enough for a tiny cloud of mosquitoes to hover around our faces and hands. "Did Mike teach you how to shoot?" I ask her.

"Yup. The important thing is, Tay, if you don't hit home the first time—and you might not—you have to get the second shot in right away; because you've made that bear pretty mad by shooting at him and he wants to kill you. So you have to make that second shot in just the amount of time it takes to pull down on the slide and squeeze the trigger—and you want to do it smooth and easy, no pauses." She cradles the gun, and fires. Then she lets down another cartridge and fires again. The sounds are huge and almost simultaneous: the two reports of the gun, the two pings as the shot hits the oil drum, making two clean holes side by side.

"Oh, Phoebe—I don't think I can do that."

"Of course you can." She empties the magazine and hands the gun to me along with a handful of red plastic, gold-bottomed cartridges. "What do you think of Robbie Mosher?"

What *do* I think of Robbie Mosher? If I'd been anywhere but here, I'd certainly have passed some sort of judgment on him by now: I would have "typed" him. I think about it; and then I say to Phoebe, "Type one: eligible bachelor without anything overtly objectionable about him. He is a bachelor, isn't he?"

"Oh, the most dangerous kind. He's in his last year of medical school before he starts his residency. Those guys are hungry to get married."

I remember my fanciful impression as I woke up after being so ill: Robbie's hand on my forehead, the soothing tone of his voice. "You're kidding! He's a doctor?"

"He's almost a doctor. Okay, I want you to take two shots in a row—no pausing in between."

I load the gun the way Phoebe has shown me, nestle it up against my shoulder, pull down the slide, and sight along the barrel. Holding my breath, I squeeze the trigger. The shotgun's kick comes as an awful surprise—just as if someone actually had booted me in the shoulder. I didn't hear the report of the gun—but I can see that I *have* hit the upper third of the oil drum, close by the holes made by Phoebe. It's rather a good feeling to have done so well on my first try. I suddenly remember that I forgot to shoot a second time.

"You're dead," says Phoebe, looking sadly at me with her Modigliani eyes.

"It's just a barrel!"

She touches my cheek. "It's a bear," she says. "Try again."

I guess it was beginner's luck: the second time I don't even hit the barrel. But I hear the report of the gun both times as it slams into my shoulder. My ears are ringing and my breast muscle suddenly cramps in protest at the repeated abuse.

I lower the gun, rotating my shoulders.

"That's right," says Phoebe. "Let the blood run into the muscle. You're just tensing up."

"Isn't shooting something that takes years to get good at, Phoebe?"

"It's a matter of nerves," she says. "This isn't precision marksmanship. Keeping your head is what matters. And that's just a decision. Either you do"—she snaps her fingers—"or you don't."

When I've taken two consecutive shots that are accurate enough to satisfy Phoebe, we walk back to the kitchen, past the grave mound, in the low-slanting, watery rays of the northern sun.

Eleven

The sea is perfectly flat—there's not a cloud in the sky. I've agreed to go out in one of the boats with Mike and Robbie to the kittiwake site at Colony II. Mike and Phoebe went out earlier to draw maps showing the locations (pictured as tiny circles) of all the nests we'll be examining. We aren't just counting the kittiwakes: we'll be monitoring their breeding productivity, which means peering into their nests to count eggs and chicks.

Our gear for this expedition includes a seventeen-foot aluminum extension ladder, three hard-hats, and a long aluminum pole—the kind that painters use for rolling paint onto a ceiling—fitted with a small hubcap.

"You're too young to remember 'baby moons,'" says Phoebe, jiggling the hubcap like a tambourine. "Bad boys used to steal them in our town—god only knows why."

We carry the equipment down to the boat together and strap everything across the bow with elastic shock cord. "You should've seen the guy's face at the paint store," says Phoebe, "when I told him I wanted to attach a convex mirror to the extension pole. I'm sure he thought I was some sort of pervert."

The baby moon is our unbreakable mirror for the nests too high up on the cliff to reach with the ladder. We'll use the extension pole to hang the baby moon over a nest so that we can peer up through binoculars from down below and count the eggs or chicks in the reflection. I'll be recording all the weights and measurements in the field notebook.

Phoebe and Strider are planning on taking Blue for a hike inland over the tussocks, up Ogoturuk Creek, to look for some hawk nests they saw there last year. She smiles cheerfully as we leave.

I have to admit my pleasure in going out, alone, with Mike and Robbie. Maybe it's part of my new sense of competence: I jump into the boat like someone who has nothing to fear.

"How's your dad, Mosher?" asks Mike once we're skimming steadily over the water.

"He's all right. Keeps threatening to come back up here someday. He wants to challenge me and Strider to a moose hunt."

"Oh, yeah? Who's his partner going to be?"

"Who do you think? Phoebe, of course."

"You're shittin' me."

Robbie laughs. "Yeah, I am. God, it's good to be back up here again. Chicago's a real hellhole."

"You're almost done, aren't you?"

"One more year. Then I'm off to San Francisco to do my residency."

"No kidding! That's where Tay's from."

Robbie looks embarrassed and pleased. "You're shittin' me," he says.

"No shit."

Robbie isn't handsome—but he has a sort of compact intensity that's very appealing. And, except when he's talking to his pals in their gross wilderness patois, he shows all signs of being both sensitive and intelligent. The only problem is that I don't seem to care any more—oh, I care, about other things. But not about finding a man; not about getting married. There's so much else at the moment that seems more important: this new-found sense of being alive; of being, somehow, potent.

Colony II is much closer up the coast than Colony IV. We land easily and pull the boat up on the beach. Our nesting kittiwakes are on one sheer cliff face rising directly above the narrow strip of shingle. Unlike the murres, kittiwakes build nests and lay more than one egg at a time. I sit for a while on the pontoon, studying the map and trying, without much luck, to find the corresponding nests. Morgie would have an easy time with this—he's used to picturing three-dimensional shapes on paper. It's hard for me to look at the cliff in its completely random juttings and depressions and find the corresponding shapes on the map. Phoebe has penciled in little land-marks, as on a treasure map: "crooked rock," "bird-shit trail," "clump of grass."

"Which bird-shit trail is she talking about?" I ask Mike, who's unstrapping the ladder from the bow. "The whole cliff is full of bird shit."

He hands me a hard-hat and sits by me on the pontoon as we pore over the map together.

Robbie walks up to us from the base of the cliff, where he's been examining the colony up close. "We've got some chicks already, Gavin—I'd say about a week old. And a lot of damage from the storm."

It must be comforting to look at the world scientifically—
to simply need to notice things, and to fit what you notice
into patterns. How much more chaotic Denny's view of
the world must be: to have to reinvent reality subjectively,
personally. What draws a person to one vision or the
other: to that obsessive search for objective reality or the
equally obsessive drive to create an alternative, to recreate
the chaos of the personal?

We walk over the uneven stones of the beach, carrying
the ladder, the pole, and the baby moon. We try to move
quietly, but the ladder rattles and scrapes, making the
birds squawk and flap their wings.

At the base of the cliff, Mike places the ladder where he
wants it, trying to find a firm footing for the base. Then he
scrambles about three-quarters of the way up. "Is this
number one?" he shouts down, touching one of the nests.
The bird sitting on it watches him, but doesn't make a
sound.

"Yup," I shout up at him. And then I ask Robbie, "Why
doesn't the bird fly away? Isn't she scared?"

"The birds up here don't see human beings often
enough to think of them as anything other than some
great big strange animal that doesn't seem to eat birds or
eggs. She—or he: you know, both the males and females
sit on the eggs—she's keeping her eye on him, but she's
not going to budge from that nest."

Mike carefully lifts the bird, leaning out from the ladder
to cup her body in both hands. She squawks in protest as
he peers into the nest and then places her gently down
again. "Empty," he shouts down at me. I write *0* by my
notation for nest number one. He picks up the incubating
bird in the next nest over on the cliff, leaning out dangerously far on the ladder. "One egg, one chick," he shouts.

Moving deftly, he holds the adult bird off to one side of the nest while he places the tiny chick, head-first, into a red bandana tied at four corners to a spring balance. He dangles his bundle in mid-air to read the weight. "Four ounces," he shouts down at us. As he replaces the bird, a couple of small rocks come skittering down the cliff face, disturbing several of the birds down below. More rocks start falling as the birds flap their wings, and Robbie pulls me over to the edge of the water.

There is something so satisfying in the pressure of his hand on my arm, in this gesture of protectiveness. "Keep your head down," he says to me. Mike stands on top of the ladder, pressed against the cliff, until the dust settles.

"Shit!" we can hear him saying. "I think we lost a chick."

Robbie and I climb over the rubble and find a baby kittiwake, still alive—a fluffball of down, pale pearl gray with darker wings. Cupping it in my hands, I can feel the warmth of its body, the pressure of its tiny heart beating. "Can we put it back?" I ask Robbie.

"We can try, but he's probably injured." I look at the chick—this fragile, live, warm thing with black beady eyes—and then up at Robbie Mosher. "He probably won't live, Tay."

I shout up to Mike on the ladder, "Will this thing hold both of us?"

He climbs down and examines the baby bird. "Oh, this one's a goner. His wing's broken." He stretches the tiny, unformed, unfeathered wing out to show us.

"Don't hurt it!" I whimper. Suddenly it matters: one small life brought into focus, lifted out of anonymity— only to die. I just know what they're going to do next: they'll "put it out of its misery."

"We'd better put it out of its misery," says Robbie, right on cue.

I stroke the chick gently. Then I hand it to Mike. "Go ahead!" I snap. "There're plenty more where he came from!"

"Look, Tay—" he says. "Would you rather we leave him here with his broken wing to starve to death?"

He's right—I'm sure he's right. It's just that . . . If this one life doesn't matter, why do any of them matter? "Why measure and weigh and count them and kill them? I don't understand what good it does in the long run."

Robbie rubs a friendly hand across my back. "Full employment for biologists."

"It's science, Tay," says Mike. "You've got to look at the larger picture. Research isn't just a matter of intuition. It takes lots of little facts, evidence . . ."

I reach out and take the bird from his hands. "I'll do it," I say to him; and walk with it down to the edge of the sea.

I understand now how the executioner feels. The chick, perhaps in a moment of comprehension, peeps shrilly and seems to look at me with terror.

Why should a baby bird be harder to kill than a spider or a fly? I can feel the tiny bones of its neck beneath my fingers, the small, furious rhythm of its heart. The bird wriggles piteously. "You eat meat, don't you?" I say aloud. Already the tears are streaming down my face. "Hypocrite!" I whisper; and then, "Dear God, forgive me!" Quickly I squeeze: I feel and hear the crunch of tiny bones breaking.

It happened right in my two hands: death. Slowly, I hear the sound of the surf again. And Mike's voice shouting down at me, "Come on, Tay. We need you up here!"

*   *   *

The next two nests on our map must be "mirrored." Near the top of the ladder, Mike holds the baby moon out as far as it will reach on the pole, trying to place the mirror so that Robbie, looking up with binoculars, can see the reflected image of the correct nest. I shout instructions from down below. "A little bit to the left—no, down; okay—hold it!"—all the time attempting to keep track of our place on the graph-paper map and to write down the number of chicks or eggs by the correct code for the nest. Mike shouts down the numbers in haste and between expletives as he's pecked by the parent birds, or pelted with bird shit, or holding his breath as the ladder shifts ominously in the sand beneath him.

When we come to the lower nests, Mike gives me a turn on the ladder. It's difficult climbing in hip-waders; I feel large and clumsy. When the chicks are put into the bandana head-first, they think they're being brooded and stay perfectly still. I find the adult birds harder to deal with. Because they're not afraid, they peck at us as they would at any other creature invading their territory; and their beaks are sharp. But all the time I'm aware of a thrilling sense of life in my hands: holding the warm, plump bird seems almost like holding flight itself.

Mike numbers all the eggs with a felt-tip pen and bands the chicks with a device that looks like a leather punch. After the first couple of hours, during which I've had moments of panic in trying to read the map, and moments of anger if Mike or Robbie express impatience with me, I begin to take pleasure in the growing efficiency with which I'm doing my job. Wet with bird shit and regurgitated fish, the red bandana has to be washed out and the spring balance recalibrated about every half hour. My khaki-green cagoule is completely limed over in white. At one point as I'm taking notes a kittiwake pelts me right in the eye, and I call time-out to wade into the Chukchi and wash.

By mid-afternoon we take a break to sit together at the edge of the sea, as far from the cliff as possible, our identically booted legs stretched out in front of us. We eat our lunch of raw cashews and raisins, apples, and chocolate. Sadly, I've joined this fraternity of cold killers. Mike and Robbie treat me differently now—just like one of the boys.

We all three look up at the distant sound of a motor, coming close fast.

"Chopper," says Robbie.

Then it swoops into view from over the top of the bluffs, passing close enough to the cliff face to start another rock slide.

"Asshole!" shouts Mike when the dust has cleared and we look up again. The helicopter dips slightly to the right, with a gesture that looks positively like a smirk, and then disappears again. The birds are in a panic, flapping their wings and squawking wildly. Either the wind from the rotors, the rock slide, or the birds themselves have knocked several eggs out of the nests and down the face of the cliff.

I look at Mike.

"I don't know," he says, shaking his head. "Maybe a pilot from one of the mining camps. They've got too much time on their hands."

"And too much booze in their rations," says Robbie.

We watch as the colony settles again, and two glaucous gulls swoop down on the ruined eggs, carrying the contents away to their own nests and their own hungry chicks.

*   *   *

Robbie and I climb over a dirt-crusted glacier to find fresh water for the canteen.

"Mike's a great guy," he says to me.

"Have you known him long?"

"Oh, about nine years. He and Strider were in the same masters program at the university. And I've known Strider since—well, I've known Strider forever."

We climb up a steeper bit, without talking. The grass is thick with wildflowers. "But I thought Strider grew up in Alaska. And you're from Chicago, aren't you?"

"No one's told you the story yet? My dad and Strider's were stationed in Hawaii together during the war—they were going on a pig hunt the day that Pearl Harbor was bombed." We sit down to catch our breath on an outcrop of rock at the edge of the glacier. "They stayed friends—you know, Christmas cards and that sort of thing. And every few years my dad would fly out to Haines to go on a hunting trip with Chuck—Strider's dad. He started taking me with him as soon as I was old enough to be trusted with a gun." Robbie looks at me, smiling ruefully. "Strider's ten years older than I am—he was all grown up by the time I met him, and he wasn't at all like he is now. Believe it or not, he was really slim and quite a good-looking fellow when he was in his early twenties. He took charge of me, and taught me how to shoot, how to survive in the woods. At home there were only my sisters . . ."

I place my hand, just briefly, on Robbie's. "I always wanted a brother, too."

"Chuck died of a heart attack, all alone out in the woods. We all flew out for the funeral. Strider stayed on with his mother for another year; and then moved to Fairbanks. Dad and I came up just about every other summer—as often as we could afford the airfare. But he doesn't like leaving Mom alone any more—her health hasn't been the best. So— you know—it's just me and Strider, now. Buddies to the end." Robbie gets up and stretches. "Well, shall we go find that water?"

He strides on up the hill. I linger behind a little, not in the mood to hurry. I find some wild onions growing in among the tussocks, eat a few of the green stems, and pick several handfuls, wrapping them carefully in my kerchief.

Robbie reappears with a dripping canteen. "Come on up for a moment. I'll show you something."

One slope above my onions, wild blueberries are growing on gnarled miniature bushes, not four inches above the ground. "We don't have time now," says Robbie, "but let's come back up here in a day or two and pick some. They're really good in pancakes."

"No—let's pick them now. Who knows when we'll have weather like this again?"

" 'Gather ye rosebuds while ye may.' "

"Something like that. Do you have anything we could put them in?"

"Voilà!" He takes two plastic sample bags out of his shirt pocket. "Boy Scout's motto: be prepared."

We both crouch down and pick the dusky fruit. The berries are tart just as they are, but they'll be a wonderful treat tomorrow, in pancakes or oatmeal at breakfast; or tonight at supper. I can't wait to show them to Phoebe.

"What do you do in real life, Tay, in San Francisco?"

"Oh, I live in Berkeley, actually. I'm—that is, I've got a temporary job as a secretary. Well, it's been temporary for about eight years now. They call me an administrative assistant, but it's really just a glorified clerical position."

"Hey, it's honorable work. What's wrong with being a secretary? Especially if you're a good one—they're pretty hard to come by."

"Oh, I'm a great secretary. It's just that, well—I always expected a lot more of myself. You know, I can write circles around most of the people whose papers I type—all they have that I don't have is a Ph.D. It's—well, sometimes it's awfully demoralizing."

"Why don't you do something else then? Go back to school and get a Ph.D. yourself."

"I keep meaning to—but somehow . . . I don't even know what field I'd want to go into. I've thought a lot about art history . . . My father's a painter—Dennis MacElroy. Maybe you've heard of him."

"Dennis MacElroy. Of course! There's a big collection of his work at the Chicago Art Institute. How amazing!"

"Well, it is amazing, in a way. But it's also a tough act to follow. My mother writes and illustrates children's books—you probably *haven't* heard of her, although she's very well thought of in her field. My parents are both tremendously successful."

"Sort of intimidating?"

I nod. "Yeah. Art history was a second choice, really—a compromise. Because I don't have any artistic talent myself. I just have—sort of a feeling for it. But, you know, I hate most of the art criticism I've read. It's so—oh, the opposite of something creative. It's—stultifying!" I pop a blueberry into my mouth.

"Strider told me that you came up here for a summer office job at James and Jacobs."

"Yeah. I'm just here by mistake, really." I stand up and stretch. All around me is emerald green grass, studded with forget-me-nots, cinquefoil, miniature lupine, and blueberries. Beyond the shadowy white of the glacier, the Chukchi is a transparent turquoise blue—I've never seen it look so lovely and benign. I walk out to the edge of the cliff for a better view.

Birds from the colony are flying over the water; and, suddenly, looking down, I can see the silhouettes of murres underneath the water. "Robbie—come look!" I call out to him. "Under the water—they're flying!"

Robbie joins me, touching my shoulder as we look down. "That's exactly how the ornithologists describe it: flying underwater."

We stand there watching; then I turn to him. "You're awfully lucky to have a calling! So many of the men I know are doing just what they want to be doing." I think of Morgie and sigh.

Robbie eats a last blueberry, then locks shut his plastic bag. "I'll let you in on a secret. What I really wanted to be was a veterinarian. But I couldn't get into a veterinary college."

"You mean it's *harder* than getting into med school?"

"Oh, much!"

"What a shame! I mean, when you're examining patients, are you going to be wishing they were horses or dogs?"

"We'll see. 'Just open wide and say Moo!'"

I start to laugh when all of a sudden I notice how close we're standing to the edge of the cliff. It makes me feel dizzy for a moment. "Come on, Robbie," I tell him, pinching part of his sleeve and pulling him away. "Mike's going to wonder what happened to us."

Twelve

~~~~~~~~~~~~~~~~~~

Dearest Morgie,

You know, the really difficult thing about being out here is that there isn't any privacy. You'd think there would be—I mean, we're in the middle of nowhere, with nothing but empty wilderness all around us. But we're cramped together into a tiny space. When I have to pee at night, I must tiptoe past Strider and a new man, Robbie Mosher, who arrived this week. Oh, you men have it easy! I have to pull down my knickers and bare my bottom to the rain and wind—and I'm always worried that there might be a grizzly bear nearby. In the daytime (while I'm on the subject of pee) I may be squatting discreetly somewhere out on the tundra, a fair distance from camp—and a small plane will fly by overhead, dive down low for a better look, and waggle its wing-flaps. Most humiliating! The other day, a small plane strafed me like that, flying so low that I hit the dirt in absolute terror. Of course, our Bill would never do that. It's hunters, mostly, I think—not the professional pilots out here.

When we have to do the other thing, we have a choice of two places: a noisome barrel set up in a dark, greasy shed filled with cast-off jeeps and god-knows-what-other trash; or the out-of-doors "throne"—it does look like a throne, except for the hole in the seat—on the southernmost point of the rising land, looking out over the sunset and the Ogoturuk delta tinted pink and gold. Oh, it's humbling and horrifying to see one's own excrement piled up (and there's no avoiding it walking to and from the throne): positively unfathomable that we carry such masses of shit around in our bodies. There's no being discreet about it. There you are in the kitchen, playing pinochle or reading; and all of a sudden you get up, tear a few feet off the roll of toilet paper, and pocket a box of matches to burn up the paper when you're through. Well, there's no mystery about where you're going. Do you think that coquetry has a chance in such an atmosphere?

Phoebe and I have a joke, that this is Camp Darwin, where evolution runs backwards. I'm turning into a fine old savage! Oh, I'm quite a sight in my panties and tennis shoes and down jacket and unshaved legs, tip-toeing past my two roommates. Often Robbie's not asleep, and just grins at me! I like this new man—he actually knows how to talk; and he reads. We've gone out on one outing together so far. No, that's not a date: but the closest one gets up here. He's a doc-tah, dahling—or will be in two years.

Can you see me as a doctor's wife, Morgie? All pink in my bathrobe, making toast and hot chocolate in the wee hours of the morning after he's come home from the hospital, bone weary? It's a pretty picture—and you know I like pretty pictures. But it's not what I want—not really. Ever since . . . Well, the idea of marriage doesn't seem to have its old appeal for me. A baby sounds lovely—yes, a beautiful, silky-skinned, smiling baby. Perhaps I'm not cut out to live in this liberated era at all—I don't seem to want what I'm supposed to want. I mean, the idea of a career is simply something that makes me feel anxious and guilty and miserable. Surely being an intelligent mother must count for something!

*I wish I knew what I wanted; I wish I knew in the way that
you know: that it were all mapped out for me, a clear shining
path. The funny thing is that I can't seem to empty my mind of
all my notions about what other people want me to be—I feel as
though I'm a horrible disappointment to everyone. Peg and
Denny have always said they don't give a damn what I do, as
long as I'm happy—and I'm quite sure they mean it. But then
along comes an eligible man like Robbie, and immediately I think,
Oh, Peg and Denny would be so pleased! But it's me talking,
really—not them at all. It's as if I've loaded myself down with all
this baggage and I want to say it's theirs, not mine.*

*Maybe I should have my head shrunk when I get back to
Berkeley. Maybe I should join a women's consciousness-raising
group. (Or go to the sperm bank and start a baby!) All I know is
this—I can't go back to the way things were. I won't fit into my
old clothes, I won't fit into my high-heeled shoes, and I certainly
won't fit into my old job. I've assumed Amazonian proportions!
Frankly, darling, I don't think Berkeley's big enough for me.*

I'm lying here like the most abject insomniac, listening to
Strider softly moan in his sleep. The wind is howling
again. Already it's getting darker each night: tonight I
used a candle as I lay here reading, trying to stop my mind
from racing. I thought I was drifting off, and blew out the
candle and settled down into my sleeping bag; but then it
started raining, and I found myself wanting to listen to the
rain and to think about things.

I've been thinking about Phoebe, and how in a funny
way I wish I *were* a lesbian. Tonight, after dinner, she
stretched and looked across at Mike and said she was
going to go to bed early. He followed soon afterwards,
saying that he wanted to polish his gun. Oh, really!

Robbie and Strider and I could barely keep from laughing. But then, later, I passed the married couple's shed on my way to pee—and I heard them making love. I hurried away to my own bed, ashamed and embarrassed and, somehow, frustrated.

Our love—Phoebe's and mine—will always be limited to this cerebral, disembodied thing called friendship. At the end of the summer, I'll go back to Berkeley (or somewhere); and Phoebe and Mike will build their house with the whalebone arches. And it all sounds terribly lonely to me, and like a terrible loss. I wish—I wish we could become sisters: blood sisters or something, the way Chessie and I did, pricking our fingers with straight-pins and rubbing the spots of blood together. But it's silly, of course. I don't even know where Chessie lives any more, or if she's married, or even if she's alive.

I read somewhere that many more twins are conceived than ever come to term: that perhaps one-third of us spend our first months *in utero* with a twin, who then mysteriously disappears—actually absorbed into our own body. And then we spend our lives looking and longing for that other self, that perfect harmony of understanding: that oneness.

Oh, the things one thinks of late at night, alone! Every time I turn around or shift my weight, this broken-down old cot creaks and groans. I finally give up and light the candle to read again. It *would* be Forster! "Only connect!" I want to. I think of the bright little bird, and can't believe that I broke its neck with my own hands. Did it die quickly? Did it die without pain? The book is getting wet—pearl-size drops darkening the page. I finally hoist myself out of bed and slip on my longjohns. Quietly I open the door. I tiptoe over to the bed where Robbie lies propped up on one elbow, looking at me.

"You're restless tonight," he whispers.

I place my hand on his arm. I squeeze so hard that it really must be hurting him. I don't want to hurt him! "Come to bed with me!"

Strider suddenly groans and turns over in his sleep. We both look over at him, silent until his breathing is steady again.

"Yes, M'am!" whispers Robbie. And then he adds quite sweetly as he climbs out of his sleeping bag, "I thought you'd never ask!" We walk back into my room and shut the door.

Robbie's feet are still warm: my own are like blocks of ice. Rather to my surprise, he holds my feet one at a time and rubs them until they're warm. Then I slip my hand inside his shirt: his chest is smooth, nearly hairless. I can feel his heart beating under my hand.

I am just drifting off to sleep. Robbie places his dry, warm hand on my forehead in just the same gesture he used when he checked me for fever, days ago.

I smile. He shifts his hand around behind my neck and kisses me softly on the lips. Then he puts his head down on my shoulder and we don't say anything. Robbie smells like woodsmoke and wild onions. I didn't use my diaphragm. Of course, I didn't say anything; Robbie no doubt assumed that I had an IUD or was on the Pill. After all, I'm a grown woman.

When I close my eyes, I see blueberries—hundreds of them, crowding close together on their gnarled stems above the permafrost of the tundra.

Thirteen

The day is fair. Robbie and Strider and I are out in the boat on a collecting expedition (even I have begun to use the euphemism). Strider sits at the stern and Robbie is sitting across from me, both of them with shotguns across their knees. We've drifted out beneath low-lying clouds to where the murres are flying back from their feeding grounds to the colonies. As the birds fly overhead, Strider says, "Duck!" and I drop my head between my legs, covering my ears. The noise of the two guns going off at once shakes the boat.

Even the best marksman, it seems, will have trouble making a clean kill of a bird on the wing. Unfortunately, when a murre is wounded, his instinct is to dive and swim as far out to sea as he can. It's such a waste when we can't recover them. My job is to lean out over the pontoon with a dip net and scoop the dead or wounded birds out of the water. The struggling birds splatter blood all over us and the boat. It is usually Strider who wrings the necks of the ones not quite dead. I don't want to do it again. The bird corpses are lined up, where Robbie has tied them together by their feet, on the floorboards.

When we have enough corpses to satisfy the needs of science, Strider revs up the motor and we skim along next to the coast. Both he and Robbie are keeping a sharp lookout for walrus carcasses on the beach—the corpses left by Eskimo hunters. Strangely, I'm the one who spots one first: a huge lump on the wet shingle, the waves lapping over it.

Robbie confirms the sight through binoculars. "This one's Tay's, old buddy! Doesn't have a head, but maybe they left the oosik."

"The whatsik?"

Strider starts to laugh, then scratches his head and lifts up his glasses to rub his eyes. "You tell her, Mosher! That's your department."

Robbie looks at me with his best good-sensible-doctor look. "The walrus penis bone, my dear."

"*Penis* bone?"

"Highly prized by collectors. Used as a club by the ancient Eskimos. Honkies like to put it on their mantlepiece."

"How long *is* it?"

Both men laugh with that stupid, self-conscious, and prurient giggle that Mike practices so annoyingly.

"Oh, shut up! I hope there *is* an oosik. I could do with a big stout club right now."

We land the boat upwind of the corpse, which looks like a huge rusty-red drum, the skin all stretched out taut with the gasses of decay. The head is gone. It doesn't look like anything resembling an animal.

"I thought that Eskimos used everything when they killed an animal."

"They used to," says Strider. "When they hunted with

spears and harpoons. Now they just fucking shoot whole-sale into a herd of walrus. When they get a good haul of ivory, they won't bother following all the wounded ones." He touches the corpse with the toe of his boot. "This is pretty typical. They took the skull and the tusks. We'll have to turn it over to see if they took the oosik."

"Or if there *is* an oosik," I remind him.

They use the paddle to turn the corpse over; but it lands on something sharp, releasing an explosive stench of gas.

"God, I don't want it!"

"Bingo!" says Robbie. I walk back down to the boat in disgust as he and Strider do whatever they have to do to cut out this part of the walrus's anatomy. They wrap it in a plastic garbage bag. It makes a surprisingly large package—the bone itself must be a couple of feet long. We head back to camp, racing ahead of the stink of rotting walrus.

"We did your butchering for you, Miss La-De-Da," says Robbie, "but you still have to clean it." Robbie seems to feel the need to keep up this pretense of field-camp bluffness with me—even though I'm certain that Strider, at least, knows we've become lovers. I don't mind, really. In a funny way, it isn't anything other than a comforting animal coziness. Oh, I like Robbie—but he's just my companion in the cave. It might have been any other man who appealed to me in some basic way—who "smelled" right. The nice feeling is one that I have about everyone in the camp now: the sense that any one of them would risk their life for me, and I for them. Really like a sort of family—brothers and sisters. Members of a tribe.

Everyone is a little worried about the weather. The sun is warm today, but the swell is too high, and the wind blowing too hard, to launch the boats. We're due for an exchange of personnel in eight days. Bill will be flying in two more field biologists—a married couple—from James and Jacobs; he'll carry Mike, Strider, and Robbie out with him on the return trip to Kotzebue. Robbie will fly on from there to Chicago. Mike and Strider will be flown out by Bill or another bush pilot to the North Slope, where they'll float the Colville River for a census of the endangered peregrine falcon population along its banks. They'll be gone for two weeks. When they return, all six of us will make the final count of murres before the colony migrates out to sea—somewhere around the middle of August. But all these arrangements depend on the clemency of the weather and the sea.

Phoebe has set up a cauldron on the beach where she's boiling the flesh off a walrus skull and tusks she and Mike found earlier; she lets me throw my oosik into the pot. Mike, Strider, and Robbie are all gathered around a broken outboard motor in one of the less sheltered sheds, which they've designated as their "machine shop"— they've posted a crude sign to that effect. The sign might as well say *Boys' Fort—Girls Keep Out*. Backwards evolution indeed! It's their playhouse.

It's lovely being alone for a bit in the kitchen. I take advantage of the solitude and the heat to fill a pot with water and heat it up for a sponge bath. "AP and C," as one of Peg's friends used to say: armpits and crotch. Refreshed and dry and quite contented, I settle myself with my book on a folding aluminum chair near the "scientific" table, where the phials and specimen bottles are kept with the dissection tools, notebooks, novels that are available for the moment, and various cans and bottles of boot wax and medicines. A small wooden box catches my eye. I scoot my chair closer over the concrete, as lazy as a cat, to open it.

Lovely! A technical drafting pen, several points, and a bottle of India ink. It reminds me immediately of Denny's drafting table—he had a whole collection of pens like this, and taught me to use them. Suddenly I can smell ink and oil paint and turpentine—all the smells of Denny's studio. I was never any good; but I enjoyed sketching while he worked away next to me at the drafting table, or nearby at his easel. We'd be holed up for hours together like that in his studio while Peg was in her studio at the other end of the house, writing or painting. She likes to say her stories out loud while she's writing, so the work is less companionable. We would all get back together again at lunchtime for bread and cheese and fruit—easy things that no one had to spend time cooking. Peg and Denny would each have a glass of wine. As a special treat, Denny made espresso coffee on an expensive machine they'd brought back with them from Europe. Denny would make me foamy cups of steamed milk for hot chocolate.

The pen looks as though it's never been used. I haven't sketched with any seriousness since I was a child, but at work, sometimes, I would use a drafting pen to fill in obscure mathematical notations that weren't contained on the symbol ball of my typewriter. There were several professors who wouldn't allow anyone else to type their manuscripts, even after I was promoted: I was known as the queen of technical typing. A useless skill, really, now that word processors are available: completely obsolete.

Just for fun, I fill the pen, and then root around for some drawing paper. I find just the thing: a bound black sketchbook, as virginal as the pen.

It's already late in the day—or evening, as it were. Well

after eight o'clock. But the light is quite lovely—a sort of watery gold. I head down for Ogoturuk, where Phoebe pointed out to me a clump of purple monkshood early this week. I hope it's still there. It's deadly poisonous, she told me—one of the larger, showier Alpine flowers. I'm sure that Peg and Denny would like to see sketches of it; of all the flowers, really.

I begin quite painstakingly, and have to start over twice when the pen point gets stuck in the paper and splatters ink. It's no good, really, without color: a line drawing of a flower! Perhaps if I were Dürer . . .

Walking back up toward the camp, I kick in a sore-headed way at pieces of ancient "camp trash" as I go along: old skeletons of murres that were eaten by Eskimos, dismembered hooves from caribou, sections of antlers; whiskey bottles with ancient-looking labels, like parchment maps; tin cans that rusted but refused to decompose; pieces of pipe and plumbing and hardware; old motors, transformers, and wires. Stuff that was once full of electricity or water or food or blood but lies empty and lifeless now.

Why not? I open the book to a fresh page and start sketching again, making an effort to work quickly, not to get hung up on tiny details. It emerges under my hand: a bird skeleton, its bones still poised ready for flight, its beak and one eyesocket directed skyward. Oh, much better material for a sketch! I turn the page as soon as the ink's dry, then draw a liquor bottle in a clump of tussock grass, carefully printing the words on the label. Again I turn the page. A child's toy—a crudely carved wooden boat—lies in a puddle of water. It must have belonged to an Eskimo child who was brought along on a hunt. The water's difficult—I muff this one, and turn the page.

The sky has begun to bloom in its sunset colors, from the fog-strewn hills to the north to the pastel-tinted waters of Ogoturuk where they're swallowed like a wafer by the sea. What I would give for some watercolors! A flock of murres flies by over the water, first in a vaguely triangular formation, then reassembling into new shapes: a cross, a crab, a warrior. I miss them for the first time: the stars! All summer long, we've had starless, twilit nights. But the seabirds mime a dance of constellations. Nothing lacks— oh, only colors; only skill! I work quickly, knowing full well that I can never capture the order and movement of the shapes, the bird-stars sailing across the sky. Perhaps, later, the sketches, however crude, will help me remember—I would like to remember this night forever. It's like trying to draw the quickly fading image from a dream.

When I get back to the kitchen, Phoebe is washing up and beans are boiling in the pressure cooker. I clean out the pen and put the sketchbook back on the table.

"Chili rellenos tonight," says Phoebe. She's already taught me how to make them from the limited ingredients we have on hand. I open a can of chilis with the can-opening blade of my Swiss army knife, and then take out the longest blade to slice them open and scrape out the yellow seeds. Phoebe slices up the last of our jack cheese and makes a batter of powdered eggs, a little flour, and water from the rusty bucket on the floor. I make the sauce out of onions, canned tomatoes, and dried herbs.

After dinner, Phoebe urges me outside to look at the moon that's risen above the sunset clouds. It hangs low over the horizon, about five times the normal size of the moon: a fat belly, a disk of light; unearthly, regal. I am too astonished to say anything—anything I could say, really, would be unequal to the sight before us. I stare at the moon, then I look, surreptitiously, at Phoebe. She seems to belong to this sight of the primeval moon, with her pellucid skin and hair much darker than the twilit night: Phoebe with her long-fingered hands that pull whale-bones out of the sea. Next to her, I feel small and complicated; the sight of the moon fills me with longing. I remember—peripherally, like the memory of a smell—a childlike perspective in a world of outsized objects, over-whelming visions of color and light (Denny, holding me in his arms, bending down so that I can smell a swollen white rose; and it floods my field of vision, swallows me as my face is buried in the overblown, unfolding flower).

"Do you want to clean bones for a while, down on the beach?" Phoebe asks me. "It's really pretty warm and there's enough moonlight for working."

I nod.

We zip up our jackets and walk through the strange moonlit trash heap, past the repair shop, past the indoor shitter, past the last outbuilding and down between the straggling rows of oil barrels to the beach, where Phoebe's cauldron is still steaming. Using a stout piece of driftwood, she lifts the boiled skull by its eye-hole and sets it, dripping and gleaming, side by side on the coarse sand with the already cleaned oosik—she must have been working on it while I was sketching.

"Thanks, Phoebe," I tell her. The oosik is about a foot-and-a-half long and a couple of inches in diameter, tapering like a baseball bat. "That'll be a conversation starter in Berkeley . . . Maybe I'll put it in my office." Suddenly I remember that I'm not going back to my old job. What *will* I do? I try to think of different places where I might live, what I might do for a living. I picture for a moment a country cottage, the oosik displayed on the hearthstone along with other souvenirs from Camp Darwin: a kittiwake skeleton, pebbles from the beach. Perhaps I'll find some tusks, too, before the summer's over.

We crouch staring at the walrus skull—its dumb massiveness protecting a tiny brain, the magnificent tusks evolving for no reason that anyone has been able to confirm. Strider told me that every marine biologist has his pet theory: the tusks are for digging in the mud, for fighting, for sexual display. Contrived for whatever reason, they're made of the most exquisite ivory, with the beauty of jewels but soft and well-suited to carving. Eskimos trace histories of the hunt on them; and now they're an inflated item for tourists, who pay hundreds of dollars for a set of tusks, and thousands if it's carved.

The Chukchi is calm tonight; above us we can hear the plashing of Ogoturuk Creek. Phoebe takes out her knife and the blade gleams silver. The smell of dead flesh and salt is strong in the damp air. We sit down on the marshy grasses, pulling the skull up between us. Phoebe begins by loosening the tusks and the teeth.

"We have to take it apart to get it clean," she explains, working. "But we'll rearticulate it in Fairbanks. Poor thing with her asymmetrical tusks wasn't good enough for the jerk who shot her." As she extracts each tooth she wipes it off, holds it up to the moonlight, then drops it in her jacket pocket.

I take out my knife and begin scraping at the cartilage at the top of the head. The sound of the knife, when it scrapes against the skull, makes my cheekbones ache. The cartilage peels away, tiny bit by bit, to reveal the white moonlit bone. Phoebe pries out the tusks and scrapes them in the tall grass. I pull the skull up, possessively, between my outstretched legs, cutting more confidently into the tough, clinging flesh.

"Are you and Robbie getting on okay?" asks Phoebe suddenly.

I look over at her, but she seems completely absorbed in her work. Of course, she would know—stupid to think that such a thing would remain secret, here.

"It's funny," I tell her. "Back home"—and suddenly it sounds inconceivable to me, a fiction I once believed in—"back home I think I would have fallen in love with Robbie—I mean claimed him for some future purpose. Made plans. But here—" I look around at the slightly moving gray and silver shadows. "Robbie's like the chocolate ration—something sweet and soothing, even salvational. But it's as if all my normal reactions—wanting to find out all about him, his past, his commitments—just aren't there."

Phoebe stops for a moment. "I had a dream once," she says, "about being a cavewoman—you know, like one of those grade *B* movies where all the starlets are running around in scanty leopard skins with their hair messed up. Only it was very simple: just the inside of a cave and a fire, where other people were gathered around, eating, sleeping. I was with Mike, but I realized that it didn't matter—it might have been any one of the other men. But it *was* Mike. We kept each other warm at night." She starts scraping again. "It was a beautiful dream—comforting. I wondered if it might even have been some sort of ancestral memory."

I peer down into the socket of the walrus's eye, and the moonlight gleams back at me. Sometimes I wonder if

Phoebe makes these things up. All along I've had the feeling that she's watching me, judging me, assessing what I've learned. A flock of birds flies by, close in to shore over the sea, calling out to each other, or just calling out to reassure themselves on their flight through the half-lit air, over the low-rolling waves. "It seems so ridiculous to me," I say to her, half testing, half in desperate earnestness, "that I'm almost thirty and I haven't decided yet what I want to do."

"Oh, most people never decide," she says, pulling away long strips of leathery flesh, then tossing them into the grass. "They take up one thing or another, or get married and have children; and they think they've decided, but all they've really done is surround themselves with a lot of things that limit their choices. They're falling down the same hole we all are, but they've just made the passage narrower. People like to see the sides of the walls while they're falling; it comforts them."

I remember, when I was a child, looking forward to the moment when I would be a grown-up—as if there were a signpost that I knew I would reach one day. I would pass it, and then it would have happened, magically: the big transition. I kept waiting to get there.

Of course, there was no one moment in time, no sign on the road. Just in the last few years, really, I began noticing that shop-girls called me "M'am." How did they know? What were they noticing that I hadn't been able to see, even though I'd been looking, watching for it in the mirror? Was it something in my voice? Something about the clothes I picked out, the food I bought in the store?

I look at my hands in the moonlight: they look old; they look ancient. Perhaps I was one of the cave dwellers in Phoebe's memory. Perhaps there is something to the idea of past connections. "I guess it's sort of ingrained—" I say out loud, "the sense that certain things are supposed to happen at certain times: growing up, choosing our work, choosing a mate. I've always felt—well, out of sync: really precocious in some ways, a real social retard in others. And then there seemed to be this big yawning gap between the way you dreamed about things and the way they turned out. You know, like the whole thing about losing your virginity: you really grow up expecting some sort of religious experience. And then it turns out to be something quick and messy, the boy you thought you loved looking at you with a stupid grin—and you're there asking yourself, 'Is that it? Did I miss something?' "

Phoebe laughs. "Yeah, that's about the way it was for me. Only just at that moment, the people I was babysitting for walked in. I *still* haven't lived that one down in Windenburg. The whole town knew the date when I lost my cherry. I'm surprised they didn't declare it a municipal holiday.

"I don't know, Tay . . . If menopause is anything like adolescence, I think I'd rather die young than put myself through that kind of torture again. It was like something out of Frankenstein. All of a sudden your body grows and bulges and sprouts hair; your metabolism goes completely bonkers. Your hormones tell you it's time to mate, and your mom looks at you solemnly, like she's about to tell you something really important, takes your hand, looks at the ground, and says that you must always keep your knees together at parties. It's like being in a Fellini movie for six years running. You're not a little kid any more: that's more than apparent from your bra size. But you don't have any more power than you did when you were small and sexless. In fact, you have less: now your parents expect you to do all sorts of chores, to earn your keep. You're not much better than an indentured servant. Your parents' friends think it's amusing to point out your pimples . . . God, what a misery!"

"I guess we should congratulate ourselves just for having lived through all that . . . Oh, I wish I had known you then, Phoebe. Wouldn't it have been fun?"

"When I was fifteen and you were seven? I don't think we would have had all that much to say to each other. Still—I guess I could have been your babysitter. But your people wouldn't have even lived in the same part of town as us. Dad was a cattle-broker. We didn't have artist friends. We didn't go to Europe—hell, we hardly ever even went to Chicago!"

We scrape for a while in silence. "Still—maybe we would have known you. Mom had a lot of . . . I guess you'd call it artistic sensibility—a lot, at least, for Windenburg. She was really famous in our county for her dahlias. She'd dig the beds and set the bulbs just like she was painting a picture." Phoebe pauses for a moment to stare out over the flat moonlit sea. "Until the accident."

"The accident?"

Phoebe sighs. "It was a hot summer day, and Mom was out in her flowerbeds weeding. The three of us—just out of diapers, really—decided to take a cold bath. We made lemonade and set our glasses around the edge of the tub. Penny knocked hers over and I stepped on the broken glass in the bathwater. Of course, my foot started bleeding, and the blood spread out in the water, and it all looked just terrible. Adelaide started screaming at the top of her lungs, even though it was my foot that was cut, and it didn't even hurt—just stung a little. Then Penny started hollering, too, just because Adelaide was—you know how kids are; and Mom heard us and came running in from the garden, not even remembering to wipe her muddy feet. Well, she took one look at her three babies there in a bathtub full of blood and she turned about as white as a ghost. I was afraid she was going to die before I could let her know I was okay."

We get up stiff-legged and walk over to the stream to rinse our knives and the teeth and the bones. "Mom never planted dahlias again after that summer—didn't even have flowerbeds. She dug them all up and planted grass instead, and hired a man to come with a big power mower to cut it down every week. She'd sit there in the living room by the big picture window watching him, and my dad would say, why don't you plant a few flowers this year? But she'd sort of shut her mouth up real tight and just shake her head. I guess she thought that God had punished her for caring about her dahlias too much."

Fourteen

Robbie and I are still in bed when we hear the plane circling, and then suddenly it's on the runway. Robbie looks at me and says, "But he wasn't supposed to come in for another four or five days." We throw on our clothes and join Phoebe, Mike, and Bill out on the gravel. Phoebe's hair is streaming; she looks angry.

"Bullshit, Mike!" she's saying. "We can't *do* the work without Ned and Kate."

Mike looks at Bill with an appeal for support. Bill looks down at the ground. "Well," he says. "All I can tell you is what they told me at the weather service: big storm coming in. I just don't think I can get you boys out to the Colville on the day we scheduled—or even that week. I'm sorry, Phoebe! I know it puts you in a bind. If your friends can get to Kotzebue before the storm does—"

"Oh, Bill—it's not your fault. God damn it. Strider, can't your peregrine project wait?"

"Fuck, Phoebe. You know better than that. The chicks

are just pipping now. You want me to write them a letter and ask them to hold off for a couple of weeks?"

Robbie looks at me. "I guess this is my last chance to get back to Chicago, Tay. I'm screwed if I don't get a head start on the reading."

Mike winks at me, then turns and walks into the kitchen. Phoebe storms in after him. "Women!" says Strider. We all file in after her.

Mike puts a cooking pot on the table, then a frying pan.

"You can't take that one," says Phoebe. "We need it here."

He ignores her and begins rummaging in the food lockers.

"That's the last of our oatmeal!" She grabs a box of Quaker Oats away from him.

Mike looks completely exasperated. "Phoebe," he whines. "Do you want us to starve to death out there?"

"I don't want you to go. It's all fucked up now without Ned and Kate. There's just too much work for the two of us to do alone."

Mike continues filling his arms with food from the locker: beans and trail mix and a huge chocolate bar.

"That's our last bar of Special Dark!" Phoebe shrieks at him.

Mike dumps the food on the table and hands the bar of chocolate to his wife. "Feeble," he croons. *"Both* contracts have to be honored. Ned and Kate will make it out in the next couple of days. And if they don't, it means the weather's too bad for counting, anyway."

"You're always doing this to me, Mike!"

"I know, I know," he says, touching her arm. "But this time it's the weather, Deedles—"

"Don't deedle me, asshole." Phoebe looks down at the

chocolate bar and I can see that she's about to cry. "Take the oatmeal," she says, thrusting it at him. Still holding on to the chocolate, she turns and walks out the door.

Bill is by now bright pink with embarrassment. He looks at Mike. "I'll bring some more oatmeal when I pick up your friends." He looks around at all three of us. "If the weather's too bad, I'll make a drop of the oatmeal . . . and more chocolate, if I can find some."

Robbie leans over and kisses me on the cheek. "I'd better pack up my gear." He goes out the door after Phoebe. Bill looks at the door and back to me, raising his eyebrows but not saying anything.

I light the stove and put up a pot of water. "Coffee in five minutes, Bill." He nods. "You don't have any letters for us, do you?"

"Darn tootin'—I almost forgot." He rummages in his inside jacket pocket. "Here you go—mail call. Two for you, Tay. There's one from your mom, Strider. And . . . let's see, this one's for Phoebe. Mike . . ."

"Oh, great," says Mike. "I don't believe this—it's a bill. Must be Pammy's idea of a joke."

My letters are from Catherine and Morgie. I slip them into my pocket. "That reminds me, Bill—I have two more to send back with you. I'll just be a moment."

Robbie's packing. He waylays me as I pass him on my way back out of the sleeping shed with Bill's handkerchief and my letters. "These are for you, Tay," he says, handing me a piece of ivory and a tiny bit of something that looks as if it might have come from the lint-screen of a drier. "That's a fossilized whale tooth—to protect you on the water. And a little bit of grizzly undercoat—I grabbed it off a bear myself—to keep you safe from you-know-what."

I take a closer look at the yellowed tooth, whose shiny

surface is crazed, like old china. The bit of undercoat is very soft. "I didn't think that Western doctors believed in this sort of thing."

Robbie shrugs. "Oh, well. It's not the sort of thing I'd want to have get around . . . It's just a bit of woodlore: 'counting *coups* on a grizzly bear.' If you can get close enough to grab some of the undercoat . . . you know, it's supposed to set up some sort of connection between you and the bear."

"Hmm," I say, looking up at the oosik hanging on the wall. "I wonder what that means in terms of me and the walrus." Unthinkingly, I wrap the tooth and the bit of fluff in Bill's handkerchief and stuff it into my pocket.

"So when're you going to come to Chicago?" Robbie asks me.

I look into his nice brown eyes. "Probably never. When're you coming to San Francisco?"

"In a year."

"Well, I'll see you then, I guess. If I'm still there."

He leans closer to me, nuzzling me in the hollow of my collarbone—the place that Balzac called "the salt cellar."

"Maybe I'll see you next summer," he says to me, "here."

"I thought this was the last year of the study."

"In Fairbanks, then. We'll go on a hunt."

"We'll see." I kiss him on the cheek. "Thank you, Robbie."

"Is that all?" I can see the reflection of my green eyes in his brown ones. "You have a boyfriend waiting for you, don't you? That guy you're always writing to . . ."

"Oh, Morgie's waiting for me, but not in the way you think. I'm just . . . Well, everything's up in the air for me, Robbie. I've got too much to figure out just now."

"Will you write to me?"

"Absolutely."

He looks at me a little longer, then smiles. "Just open wide and say, 'Moo!' "

"Moo!" I say to him. He kisses me on the mouth.

The plane has already turned around to taxi down the gravel when Phoebe comes running out of her sleeping shed, waving the chocolate bar. "Mike!" she calls—but her voice is drowned out in the sound of the motor. Bill leans out of the window and salutes; Mike and Strider wave as the Otter rolls by on its rickety wheels. Blue is barking, and Phoebe is still calling out, "Mike, you asshole, take the chocolate!" when the plane rises up into the air, gets smaller and smaller, and then disappears.

Blue stops barking. We can suddenly hear the waves and the sound of the creek. Phoebe tears open the paper wrapping of the chocolate bar and opens the foil enclosing it. There is a loud sound of breaking. She hands a piece of chocolate to me and breaks off another one for herself. "Come on," she says, slinging her arm around my shoulder. "Help me move my stuff over to your shed. You, too, Blue!" Cavalierly, she breaks off more chocolate and feeds it to the dog, who yelps with pleasure.

Phoebe takes the bunk that Strider slept in, and Blue settles in on the one that nominally belonged to Robbie. When I climb into my sleeping bag I find a pair of Robbie's underwear at the bottom—dirty underwear that he'd worn for a week. I toss it out onto the floor. Maybe I'll wash it, later, when I do a bucketful of my own clothes.

And then I see how ridiculous I'm being. What am I going to do, send his jockey shorts to Chicago? They'll go into Phoebe's next campfire on the beach.

My sleeping bag smells like Robbie; smells like sperm and unwashed panties and wild onions and smoke. It takes me a long time to fall asleep. And then I wake up in the darkness with the memory of a dream. I was rushing for a train, but I had too many suitcases and they were all made of stone. They were impossibly heavy as I tried to drag them to the platform. The engine started, the wheels were turning, the whistle screeched, and the train rushed by in a whirl of steam and smoke while I was still calling out, falling down, dragging my luggage. One of the suitcases hit the ground and snapped open. I stared down into it, unbelieving: there was nothing inside but dust and bones.

The plastic windows collapse inward and then explode as if about to burst. I sit up in bed in the darkness and fumble for a match. It hasn't been so dark all summer.

"Tay!" I hear Phoebe's voice from the next room. "Tay, I think you'd better move in here."

I climb shivering out of my bag and carry it with the candle into the larger room. Blue has vacated Robbie's bunk in favor of lying at the base of Phoebe's sleeping bag. I spread out on the second cot, pulling the bag up around my shoulders. Phoebe and I stare at each other in the candlelight as the rain begins to drum against the roof and the windows like a thousand hammers.

The first leak sprouts in a spot near the foot of my bed, then another one starts by the door. The rain weeps in at the window. I get up again to move my bunk out of the way; Phoebe puts the drip-pots into place and dives back into her bed, shivering. Like volume turned up on a stereo, the rain grows louder; the drips come closer. We don't bother saying what is suddenly obvious: Bill won't be able to land in this weather. There will be no appearance by Ned and Kate with fresh provisions and help for launching the boat. There will be no launching the boat at all; no productivity work at the colonies.

I lie in my bag thinking about the birds out there: row upon row of them, all turned inward toward the cliff, sheltering the chicks, dripping and gleaming; the cliffs black and sodden, slimy with bird-shit and mud. I think about the glaucous gull in the matted-down grasses, and of the weasel in its passages underground.

"Oh, God!" wails Phoebe. "I forgot to fill the water buckets. Ogoturuk's going to be liquid mud before morning."

The thought of not having enough fresh water is actually enough to get me out of my sleeping bag. I walk on cramped, cold feet to the back room where my clothes are folded on the shelf.

"What're you doing?" calls Phoebe above the noise of the rain and wind.

"I'm going to go out and fill the buckets."

I can hear Phoebe laughing in the next room. When I emerge with my clothes and foul-weather gear on, she's also out of her bag and halfway dressed. "You're full of surprises, Tay. Wait till I tell Mike."

The outside door explodes open when we turn the knob. We run through the unaccustomed darkness and the wet and cold to the kitchen, Blue barking and biting at raindrops behind us; then rest for a moment before we each grab a bucket and head out the door again. Phoebe holds my hand as we slide and scramble down the talus bank to the creek. At the gravel spit we crouch down to fill our buckets. The creekwater is black and icy cold. Every shape in the darkness looks like a bear.

By the time we reach the kitchen again, our teeth are chattering. Phoebe's face becomes visible suddenly as she lights the Coleman lantern; her lips are blue.

The kitchen is ugly from the packing and arguments of the day before. The wind-up alarm on the scientific table shows four o'clock; but we're both too geared up now to go back to sleep. One of the windows has torn in the wind, and rain is seeping in like blood from a wound. Phoebe lights the heater, and I repair the window, wiping the plastic dry and bandaging it with silver tape. We nibble on pilot biscuits and peanut butter while a pot of water boils on the stove for tea. The windows are soon completely fogged. Phoebe curls up with *Moby Dick*—the only one of our novels she hasn't read yet.

Rummaging around in the food lockers, I find flour and cornmeal and a few packets of yeast—Phoebe told me earlier that she always includes yeast on the chance that someone might feel energetic enough to start a sponge for sourdough pancakes: hopes are high at the beginning of the field season. I mix two cups of the cooled-down tea water with yeast and honey, letting it rise in a tin pot on top of the heater, covered with a paper towel. When the mixture starts to bubble, I add salt and some whole wheat flour and oil and stir in white flour until it's thick and sticky. Then I roll up my sleeves to knead the dough, clearing and cleaning a place on the kitchen table where a few nights before we were dissecting murres. The rain blows, the windows pop, and the wind bellows in the stove. The dough feels like a baby beneath my hands, warm and round, fragrant and smooth. I oil the pot and turn the dough over once inside it, placing it on the heater again to rise.

Phoebe turns her attention to the unpacked gear and begins to put things away. I wipe the table and sweep, screw down the lids of food jars, and wash our dishes, using as little water as possible. The wind keeps changing direction, coming first from the north, then whipping around from the west, from the sea. I spot my sketchbook on the scientific table.

"Will you promise not to laugh if I show you some drawings I made?" I ask Phoebe. I drink tea while she looks through my "trash pictures."

"Do you think I might try drawing you while you're reading?" I ask her as she hands the sketchbook back to me.

"Why not? Clothes on or off?"

"Well, off, I guess, if you'll be warm enough . . . It's bound not to be very good, Phoebe. Not worth you catching a cold."

"Oh, I've always wanted to make a sacrifice for art."

"Hmm—not me . . ."

"Well, I guess you wouldn't, growing up the way you did. You've probably made your fair share of sacrifices to art already."

"Oh, don't get me wrong, Phoebe! Peg and Denny are wonderful. They just never treated me like a child—and I never *got* it about being a child. I mean, I didn't understand why my paintings and drawings looked so crude next to theirs . . . I gave up on art as a vocation pretty early on."

"Well, something must have rubbed off. I like your pictures."

I shrug my shoulders, but of course I'm pleased. "I make sketches at museums sometimes. It's a great way to look at something closely—Peg and Denny taught me that much. Sometimes, when I was traveling with them, it was also a good excuse to sit down and rest my feet . . ."

"Didn't you ever call them 'Mom' and 'Dad'?"

I feel embarrassed all of a sudden. "I guess not. Oh, maybe when I was just learning to talk . . . I don't know—everyone else called them Peg and Denny. . ."

Phoebe slips her arms out of her flannel shirt, leaving it tucked in. She pulls her turtleneck off over her head, and unfastens her bra. Then she settles in with her book again. "How's that?" she asks me.

Phoebe is breathtakingly beautiful like this—a fit subject for Rubens or Botticelli: her pale, fine-grained skin, her gorgeous breasts and shoulders. "I wish it were Denny drawing you and not me."

"Someone should teach you to stop putting yourself down, Tay. You're— Well, I've been pretty amazed at the way you've adjusted up here. Mike and Strider had a bet going that you were going to flag down a plane and hitch a ride back to Kotzebue in the first week . . ."

"Well, I might have; I almost did."

I smooth out a fresh page for Phoebe. The drawing starts to grow beneath my hands. Again I find myself wishing for color. I draw the plaid fabric of the shirt that's draped around her waist. I leave her black hair in outline. It's true: when you draw something, you possess it. Phoebe is mine forever now.

When I'm finished I hold my face close to the drawing to blow on the ink. When it's no longer shiny, I hand the open sketchbook across the table to Phoebe, who's idly passing her finger over a small pimple on her chest. "Nice!" she says. "I like it."

She puts her clothes back on; I put my sketchbook back on the scientific table.

*   *   *

The room fills with the smell of warm yeast when I punch down the bread. There's no rolling pin, so I press the dough flat with the heels of my hands, and punch out circles with a coffee cup. The dough circles rise on a piece of aluminum foil covered with cornmeal.

Phoebe has fallen asleep at the table, her head resting against the wall. Blue walks over to me and places his head on my lap; I stroke his smooth black coat and smile down into his quizzical eyes. A sort of domestic bliss settles down over us: the kitchen assumes the proportions of an entire world, complete.

The smell of the muffins, as I lift them golden brown from the skillet, wakes Phoebe from her slumber. She stares at them, blinking. "They look just like the ones you buy in the store! I didn't know that anyone actually *made* English muffins."

There are scads of them—an abundance of muffins. We split several of them open, one at a time, to spread them with butter and strawberry jam. When we've eaten our fill, we pile the rest of the muffins on a plate in the center of the table, then drink some more tea. One at a time we run out into the wind and cold to relieve our bladders. Opening the storm door to walk back into the kitchen is like returning home: the warmth, the smell of fresh-baked bread.

I can imagine Phoebe and myself as old ladies, living in a cottage by the sea with a vegetable garden and lots of cats and artifacts from Camp Darwin hanging on the walls. I don't know what comes in between. It's all a blank to me, a mystery. But I can see us clearly when we're old: twins, so long lost to each other; reunited at last.

Fifteen

~~~~~~~~~~~~~~~~~~~~~

Dear Catherine,

Your letter came as manna from heaven (quite literally, in a small plane that dropped into camp from the sky). I can't tell you how much I laughed over the Cootie's crise d'amour. My God—someone should write a television sitcom based on the college! And I'm so sorry to hear about poor Ellen—it seems that I'm hearing about more and more breast cancer. Did people simply not talk about it before, or is it some kind of epidemic? Your support is going to be so important to her in the next few months . . . It strikes me so hard these days that there is no safety. Ellen was always so careful about everything. It makes one fatalistic. Perhaps there really are numbers on the wall somewhere, one for each of us; and when your number's called . . .

Oh, I'm getting morbid again! It's this latest storm we've been having—it's the fourth day today, no respite. Even Phoebe grows tiresome. I've read everything—today I read the newspaper that Phoebe used for packing the food boxes (that's how desperate I am). We're running out of letter-writing paper.

Everyone else has flown off for one reason or another, leaving *me and Phoebe alone. We've discovered that we both know quite a few of the Child ballads that Joan Baez used to sing—you know, the ones with thirty verses each. Phoebe and her sisters used to sing them in three-part harmony. So I make my best attempt to stay on key with the melody while Phoebe sings the alto line. The effect is actually quite stupendous with the background percussion of rain and wind. We've sung ourselves hoarse. Phoebe's five foot, ten inches of restlessness; she's gone down to the beach this morning to look for anything interesting that might have washed up on shore. The weather's so bad that even Blue has to be urged outside.*

What I wouldn't give for a lovely fresh fruit salad: watermelon and grapes, pineapple, cantaloupe, strawberries—oh, strawberries! Our main food these days is rice and beans. I think I'm getting fat on rice and beans. I attempted an apple pie (canned apple slices, Crisco crust) in our Dutch oven—it didn't taste much better than one might have expected. English muffins have been a success, but we're out of yeast. I know we're hard up—when an animal runs or walks by, my first thought is to wonder what it tastes like.

I'll leave this for now in hopes of something more interesting developing than my gastronomical fantasies.

I tuck my unfinished letter into my pocket. The only book in camp I haven't read (apart from Strider's trash adventure novels) is the three-inch-thick black volume called the *Darwin Report*—a compilation of the "camera-ready" pages produced by the geologists, biologists, botanists, and anthropologists who've been under contract to study this section of coastline. Even though the whole notion of major mining operations in this area has more or less been scrapped, Darwin has continued to be a magnet for scholarship because of the sheer volume of work that's been done here already: studies of the bird and insect populations, studies of the plant communities, the marine life, the Eskimos, the weather, the temperature, the wind.

Flipping through the book, I pause at the sketches of prehistoric Eskimo hovels, with crosses marking the location of objects that were found there. These are documented in separate drawings: a whalebone needle, a crude wooden spoon, a piece of stone chipped into a point. Funny to think that we're adding our own garbage, our own anthropological trail that later scientists or explorers may follow. The report of the surviving army scientist who overwintered with his partner is couched in the driest scientific terms: "Chief Scientist Matthewson expired on January 11, 1959, after prolonged exposure at temperatures below minus 40F. First-aid procedures were followed but failed to achieve a recovery." The author neglects to tell what he did with the body—but I suppose that he couldn't have buried it, not in wintertime in the frozen ground. It must be an Eskimo, then, in the grave mound.

The black book itself smells like dampness and decay, like an ancient family Bible, like a book of the dead. I hold it suddenly with a sense of fear: what will our report say? I think about Ellen, my acquaintance from work who has cancer now. About Robbie at medical school in Chicago, a bright circle of light inside a ring of poverty and anger. And Mike and Strider on the Colville, where it may well be snowing now. Of Bill, flying his tiny plane through some of the fastest-changing weather on earth, over land where no one would find him if he crashed, if he stalled. I think about Peg and Denny, both in their seventies now. Something could happen and I wouldn't be there; they'd have no way to reach me.

The storm door bursts open, letting in a blast of cold air.

Phoebe slogs through from the vestibule, shedding her raincoat, breathing hard. She looks all right, at least. Her color is high from the cold outside. "Did you find anything?" I ask her.

"Just a float." She takes a fragile-looking glass globe out of her pocket—about the size of a grapefruit, a beautiful aqua-blue.

"Pretty!"

"The Japanese use them for their fishing nets. Can you imagine—it floated all this way without breaking. You can have it, if you'd like. I have several already." She wipes her wet face with her sleeve, then notices the open book on my lap. "Have you read the paper on the red-throated pipit?"

"Haven't run across that one. You know, someone should teach these scientists how to write."

Dripping rain onto the page, Phoebe runs her index finger down the table of contents. "Here . . . page 651. The guy who wrote it was out here with us one summer. Traveled all the way up from Edmonton at his own expense just to look for it."

"For what?"

"The red-throated pipit. He'd run across some study that mentioned a couple of sightings here. Usually you just see them in Asia. A freak wind, maybe. Some sort of mix-up during migration. You know, even birds get lost sometimes."

"Did he find it?"

"Nope. He got mighty wet trying, though. Both sightings were made during storms, and this Canadian thought that would be the best time for him to go out looking, too."

"Sounds awful." Suddenly I wish I'd never opened the

Darwin Report at all. I could have put Sno-Seal on my boots instead. Or finished my letter to Catherine. Or made some pancakes. I close my eyes, knowing what Phoebe's going to say next.

"I've about had it with sitting around here on my can. What do you say to hiking on up the creek and looking for that old pipit?"

"Phoebe, it's freezing out there! And—I'm about to get my period. What if a bear gets wind of me?"

She laughs. "I know. We've synchronized. We'll really smell up a storm—probably have half the bears on the northwest coast in a perfect frenzy!"

"That's not funny."

"You know how to shoot now. We'll take the gun. And Blue—he can be bear-bait."

"Phoebe, I think your head is cracked."

"Oh, come on, Tay. Can't you just see Mike's face when we tell him we've seen the red-throated pipit? He'll shit a brick. Strider won't talk to me for a year, and that guy in Edmonton will probably cut his throat."

"Sounds really cheerful. Take an aspirin, Phoebe. I think you have cabin fever."

Phoebe sits down on the other folding aluminum chair right next to me so that our knees are touching. She smells like the cold salt air. "You know that big white patch that looks like a glacier as you're looking northeast over the creek? That's cotton grass—the most amazing stuff. You can make a sketch of it. You can bring some back with you."

"It's too wet for sketching, Phoebe."

"I'll show you the place where the rough-legged hawks are nesting! The adult birds'll fly out over our heads and scream at us—you'll get a really close look at them."

"Maybe when the weather clears . . ."

"Please, Tay! We'll start getting on each other's nerves if we don't get some exercise."

"What do you mean, 'start' . . ."

Phoebe begins to say something, but I cut her off, placing my hand on her shoulder. "You'd better show me a picture of this bird so I'll know what I'm looking for."

She pats me on the cheek with her ice-cold hand, then shows me a sketch of the pipit in her field guide.

"It's not even in color," I complain.

"None of the accidentals are. It looks just like this, but there's a blush of red—here—at the throat."

"How big?"

Phoebe holds out her hand. "About half this size."

"Jesus, Phoebe. How're we supposed to find a tiny thing like that in all this weather?"

I load the gun and sling it over my back. I'm so hot by the time I'm bundled up that I find myself urging Phoebe out the door.

Ogoturuk is so swollen that we have to hike about half a mile out of our way, down to the beach, to where a driftwood timber, half-submerged, bridges the creek. The log is green and slippery-looking, but Phoebe walks across as lightly as someone in ballet shoes, the swift water splashing up past her knees. Blue unceremoniously dives into the water and swims across, barking taunts at me from the other side.

I put one foot out from the shore, and then force the other foot to follow. The weight of the gun on my back makes it difficult to keep my balance—and I'm miserable at this sort of balancing act anyway, despite the years of ballet. I start out slowly, one careful step at a time. Then I slip. Five quick drunken steps propel me across to the other side. The thought of having to cross again going the other way makes me feel sick at my stomach.

The rain is all around us like a net and a symphony. It beats down on the hoods of our cagoules, on the sodden tundra, and into pools of bogwater. The rain-filled wind blows up under our parkas, inflating us like dark green balloons. At each step the wet ground sucks at the soles of our boots like a morbid kiss.

Phoebe leads us further south and away from the creek, where I'm surprised to see some ruined corrugated metal walls and a long gravel strip, harder packed and wider than the runway at Darwin. We sit downwind of one of the walls, more or less out of the rain. Phoebe takes off her waders and changes to her tennis shoes, folding down the tops of her boots. The rain provides a lively percussion against the metal walls while she explains that this was the old runway, built to bring in the larger vehicles and building materials. Everything had to be hauled or driven overland from here to the camp.

Phoebe peels an orange for us while I change into my sneakers; the rind sprays its perfume into the damp air. The orange itself is frostbitten, disappointingly dry. We chew each piece slowly. Blue sniffs at the rind, his nose twitching.

Free of my heavy waders, I feel light and energetic by the time we start again. We hike over lush green hills. When I grow used to wet feet and the watery, blustery air, I begin to see the beauty of the landscape—even the beauty as seen on such a day. We come upon another creek cascading toward us in a series of waterfalls. The color everywhere is green; even the light is green-tinged.

The waterfalls and the creek are just another density of water in a watery world. The rain drips off the ends of our noses; it gleams on Phoebe's teeth when she smiles. Blue shakes himself off and is immediately soaked again.

To amuse myself as I stride along beside Phoebe, I remember the articles of clothing that are folded in boxes and stored in the closet in my flat in Berkeley. Each remembered garment makes me smile as if recalling the punchline to a joke. A maroon silk blouse with mother-of-pearl buttons strikes me as the funniest of all. How could two such opposite disguises coexist in the same lifetime? I try to remember the actual feel of silk against my skin. Even to remember my skin as it was, clean and smooth, dry and warm, rubbed with expensive lotions. What if the blouse were suddenly here, as if I had just picked it up from the dry cleaners in its long plastic covering? It would be the plastic that would be more useful to me here than the blouse! The silk would melt in the rain; the buttons would join the complicated coarse sand of the shingle beach.

I try to imagine Peg and Denny here in this landscape with me; to see with their eyes. Peg would find a story in the soft rolling hills with shallow scrapes in them where bears have bedded down for the night. I can imagine Peg's lean, finely-wrinkled face staring transfixed over the scenery. How cold she would feel! I send the thought of Peg away, back to her warm house, to Denny's arms. What if Morgie suddenly appeared, there, over the crest of that hill? I can see him in a tweed jacket, a large black umbrella sheltering him. He waves, uncertainly, as if he's not really sure that it's me; then rushes off on some urgent business of his own. The Cootie peers up out of a clump of willows, waving a sheaf of papers. "Tuesday, my dear! I need it on

Tuesday at the latest." But his face melts in the rain; the papers fly up into the wind and scatter.

Blue is at my side suddenly, butting me with his forehead; I reach down to pat him with my gloved hand. How many different ways there are to look at things! Myriad points of view, frames of reference, interpretations of reality. Reality! I've gone through my life like a horse wearing blinders, incapable of seeing anything but the little slice of existence directly in front of me. I've never learned to see! What secrets would a meteorologist read in the sky now? What would a geologist know just by walking over the spongy surface of the hills? What is it that Blue smells when he holds his nose in the air and it quivers and his eyes flash gold? How does Phoebe remember the location of the hawks' nest; what are her markers in this vast, watery landscape? How would a composer gather up the sounds of the rain, the wind, the creek, our labored breathing, the suck of our shoes, and organize it all into music?

I veer off to my left, catching sight of something white on the greenness of the next hill. As I get closer, the white patch assumes a shape: a pair of caribou antlers, stained magenta and green by moss, nibbled by calcium-hungry ground squirrels. I drape them around my neck, the broadest "fingers" curving out from each of my shoulders. I want to carry these things with me into the future. My future! It's all blurry and blank—amorphous, terrifying, unknown. I remember something my classics teacher at Berkeley said about the ancient Greeks' notion of time: the past is in front of you, discernible in all its detail. It's the future that walks at your heels, unseeable; about to catch you.

Sixteen

At the nest of the rough-legged hawks, the female flies over our heads screaming while we look up at her through binoculars. It seems so astonishing that all this life is going on, all around us—and would be going on even if we never bore witness. It makes me feel small in the landscape, off-center. What experiences have I missed because I haven't been in the right place at the right time? It's not all for my benefit, this pageant of nature: the sunset clouds, the oversized moon, the wildflowers; the passion of this mother bird, her fierce, operatic performance in the sky overhead. It's all unfolding, with or without me; with or without Phoebe.

Soaked through and walking heavily, we approach the cotton grass that looks so inviting with its thousands of white puffs sticking up through the marshland, looking like a featherbed, beckoning us to lie down. We come to the very margin of the cotton-grass meadow. It's growing in water—like rice paddies: black, freezing bogwater.

Two small birds fly up out of the rushes, twittering. At

the first flash of red I raise my binoculars; but the birds disappear into the cotton grass.

"Phoebe!" I whisper.

She starts walking off downstream. "Redpolls," she says over her shoulder. "Come on, Tay. I'm starting to get really seriously cold."

We stop once to scrape at the dirty crust of a glacier and suck at handfuls of clean snow. Phoebe brings the last of the bittersweet chocolate out of her pocket; the sight of it makes my cheeks water.

"I had a dream last night," says Phoebe as we stumble homeward from the old landing strip after changing into our waders. My tennis shoes, suspended by their laces from the antlers, swing to and fro like pendulums.

"Mike and I were driving in a car, at night—I guess I was driving and Mike was in the passenger's seat. It must have been the South—a hot, dark evening and the sound of insects, thousands of them, in the swamps by the side of the road. June bugs, crashing against the windshield. And then all of a sudden it was clear blue stars falling into the windowpane. The car seemed to stay still while the road rushed by and the stars fell against the window . . . like rain."

"It's not too hard to figure out what inspired that one . . ."

"Yeah, of course—the rain. But this had a different feel to it. Sometimes I think . . . Mike sort of has this way with his thoughts; a way of settling them down over other people. Sometimes I wake up in the middle of the night while he's in the field, and his thoughts are all over me, sticking to me, like the goo after making love." We walk on a little ways in silence. "The only thing gets me back to sleep then is a little whiskey. It's like thought-thinner—melts it away."

Suddenly Blue goes all tense, barks hoarsely, and tears down to the creek, his hindquarters shaking.

We stop for a moment, waiting for Blue in the rain. "Do you think they're all right?" I ask Phoebe.

"I guess so. I wish they'd had some whiskey with them. There's nothing like whiskey for helping you fall asleep when you're cold."

There's a motor sound in the distance, rattling in the sky: a helicopter shredding the rainclouds with its strange loud-soft, throbbing heartbeat sound.

I have to shout above the noise. "Do you think it could be—what're their names? Ned and Kate?"

"Not in a chopper. Must be some geological survey people. Or miners. Helicopters are too expensive for the likes of us."

Then the helicopter disappears, past our camp, and we can hear the rain and wind again. From down the hill we hear Blue bark twice, and then a sharp squeal of pain. He trots back up the bank to us with something small and limp hanging from his jaws. Two tiny red drops of blood appear on his muzzle and drip downward, mixing with the rain.

"Bad boy!" says Phoebe. "Drop it, Blue! Bad dog!"

Blue looks at us pleadingly and then drops a dead baby ground squirrel at our feet. Its back is broken. Blue wags his tail.

"He thought you'd be pleased, Phoebe. Look at him!"

She grabs on to his collar, then throws the tiny corpse as far away from us as she can, back in the direction we've come from. "Stay!" she says to Blue. "I guess I should've let him eat it. Strider would've. It's all right, Blue," she says, patting him on the flank. "Were almost home."

Phoebe is already a dozen paces ahead of me when I remember having to cross the half-submerged timber. "Phoebe—" I call out to her, catching up. "I'm too tired to hike all the way back downstream. How about if we try fording the creek up here instead—someplace where it's narrow."

"We're bound to get soaked."

"We're *already* soaked. We'll be changing out of our clothes in half an hour."

We walk to the edge of the bank and look down. Blue apparently likes the idea: he clambers down the bank and belly-flops into the water, where the current catches him. For a moment he's floating downstream, just his head showing, bobbing up and down like a seal. Then he scrambles, slightly dazed-looking, onto the opposite shore. He shakes himself off and and wags his tail, barking at us to follow.

"Not my style, Blue!" Phoebe shouts down to him. "I don't know," she says to me. "I think we should hike the extra half-mile to the bridge."

I climb down the bank to get a closer look. Ogoturuk's gone completely muddy. It's impossible to tell how deep the water is.

"I'm going to give it a try," I shout up at Phoebe. I take a couple of steps into the water.

"Be careful!" she calls down to me. I wave and walk in further, up to my knees.

The current is pulling hard, tugging at my feet. I grip the antlers at the side of my head for balance. My tennis shoes are swinging wildly to and fro.

The water rises above my knees. I pull up the bottom of

my cagoule and tie it beneath my breasts. I hitch the gun up higher on my shoulder.

Suddenly I'm in the middle of the stream. My sneakers are skimming the water, brushing the surface like a soft-shoe dancer. I take another step, but the bottom is missing. Icy water pours down into my boot. I can't believe I've been so stupid. Groping, my foot finds a place to rest, deep at the bottom of a hole.

Both boots are full, as if packed with ice. My jeans are soaked up to my waist, my hands hang limply over the antlers. I can see Blue, a black shape, dancing along the shoreline.

The creek looked so narrow from up above. It might as well be the Mississippi now. My water-logged, ice-packed, aching legs are too heavy—there's not enough weight up above to counterbalance them. I stagger forward like the Commendatore in *Don Giovanni*, a stone statue trying to walk. All the feeling is gone below my waist. All I can think about is getting back to the kitchen: something hot to drink; some food. The heated air of the room.

Finally the water's shallower; it pours from me as I rise like a surfacing submarine. I am too stiff to bend—I simply fall on my butt on the gravel, the water swirling in eddies around me. I can see Phoebe, high above on the opposite bank. She clasps both hands above her head with the gesture of a boxer who's just won a fight. Then she points to herself and points downstream, toward the bridge.

I can't blame her, after watching me practically gobbled up by the water. I wave goodbye, then pull off my boots, one at a time, holding them upside down. My feet feel broken. They bring to mind some photographs I once saw of the bound feet of Chinese women—feet mutilated into the shapes of clubs, toeless and crippled, bound in rags and twine. I try to stuff them into my tennis shoes; finally, I have to take the laces out completely before they'll fit.

It's only with tremendous difficulty that I hobble up the final stretch of tussocks and gravel in the rain. Blue is leaping in the air at my side, in front of me, and back again. He's scratching and whining at the storm door before I get there. I push it open and dump the antlers and my boots in the vestibule. Then I stand for a moment in the darkness, listening to the sound of laughter inside.

I push the door open. There's a stranger in the kitchen, sitting all by himself on a bench facing the door. He must be in his late thirties, clean-shaven with short hair and sharp features. I don't like his face. He's wearing a turquoise stud in one ear. Whatever he was laughing at trailed off into desultory sniggers at my entrance. He fools with a half-empty whiskey bottle on the table while looking me up and down. My sketchbook is open on the table; my drawing of Phoebe is smudged with strawberry jam. It looks as though the man has singlehandedly eaten the rest of our English muffins. I notice his hands: they're grotesquely small, like the hands of a child or a doll. He has the expressionless eyes of someone addicted to tranquilizers.

I take this all in, dripping and shivering. Type four: red lights, danger. Man of unknown background, character, motivations. Hope for the best, expect the worst. I shift the gun on my shoulder. A pool of water has gathered beneath the dripping hem of my cagoule. I nod at him. "Evenin'."

He smiles at me. It's the smile of someone who grew up poor—stained, crooked teeth. "Evenin', M'am."

"Get lost in the storm?"

"You might say that. One helluva storm."

He's slurring his words. The glazed look in his eyes is from the liquor—I guess it's from the liquor.

I don't have all that many choices, really. I can't send him back out into the storm. I remember something from a medieval history class—how strangers in the Arab world would grab the center pole in the tent of their host as a guarantee of hospitality and safe conduct. It didn't matter if your host was your enemy.

I sigh, resigned to being sociable. "My name's Tay MacElroy."

He's sniggering again.

"Something funny about that?'"

"Oh, my name's Captain Taylor."

"Well, it does seem like a coincidence, doesn't it?" I ease the gun off my shoulder, and pull my dripping cagoule over my head. I take off my watch cap and squeeze it out into the sink. "We thought you might have been our menfolk, coming back." I start some water on the stove for beans, and another, smaller pot of water for tea.

Captain Taylor has turned on the bench to watch me. "Where's your friend?"

I'm quite uncomfortable all of a sudden. I remember the sketch of Phoebe, half-naked, the lines of her body being traced by this stranger as he ate our muffins and jam and drank his whiskey.

"She crossed the creek downstream of me. She'll be along any moment now." I pause. "We're expecting our men any time now—as soon as the weather settles down enough."

He pours some whiskey into a cup and offers it to me. "Oh, this weather's gonna take a long time to settle down. Could be days."

I take the cup from him and try a swallow of the whiskey. My feet and legs have begun to thaw. They hurt deep down in the bones.

Captain Taylor takes a pull of whiskey from the bottle. There's nothing else I can do until the water boils; so I sit down on one of our beach chairs. I feel as if I could fall asleep, right here, sitting up in the chair. I should change into dry clothes.

"Looks as though you two had a nice long hike," says Taylor. He scoots his bottom along the bench until he's sitting close enough to touch me.

Blue has settled underneath my chair; he turns and sighs as Taylor moves closer to us. "Jeez, it's hot in here," I say, rousing myself. "Would you do me a favor and drop about a cup of beans into the water when it starts to boil, and lock on the lid of the pressure cooker? I'm going to get into some dry clothes. The beans are in the food locker over there . . . where you found the jam."

I pick up the gun; I take the cup of whiskey as a treat for Phoebe. "And, Captain— You'd better play by our rules while you're here. No bullshit. I mean it."

I don't wait for an answer. Blue follows me as I walk out the door.

After crossing the gravel once more in the rain, I shed the gun and peel off my clothes in the back room, near my shelves. When I'm all undressed and towelled off, I reach up shivering for some dry underwear.

Nothing is where it's supposed to be. I take a better look around. One of my bras is spread out on the bed next to one of Phoebe's.

So that's what he was sniggering about, the bastard. I

dress quickly. If only there were a window from which I could watch out for Phoebe, make sure she comes here first instead of to the kitchen. I drag a packing box over to the door, wrap my sleeping bag around my shoulders, and sit down. If I listen carefully, I'll hear her footsteps on the gravel through the sound of the rain and wind.

I'm falling asleep again. I don't realize it until Blue starts barking. And then I jump up and open the door for Phoebe. But it's Taylor instead, standing out in the rain. "Can I talk to you?" he asks me, shouting over the noise of the wind.

I let him stand there. The rain is flattening his hair down against his forehead. I pull the sleeping bag closer in around me. "I want to talk to *you*," I tell him. "You've got a thing or two to learn about minding your own business, Mr. Big-Shot Helicopter Pilot."

Taylor looks down at the ground. A drop of rain hovers at the end of his nose. It's shaken off when he looks up at me again. "That's what I want to talk to you about. I'm really sorry. I mean, I don't know what came over me."

"Apology accepted. But I'd advise you to sober up. Because the first patch of blue I see in the sky, you're going to hightail it back to wherever you came from."

Wearily, Taylor favors me with a military salute. "Yes, M'am!" he says. "I'll bring you some beans when they're ready, if you want. Or maybe you'll forgive me enough to eat with me."

He doesn't turn to go back. He just stands there in the rain, getting wetter and wetter. I gaze past him out onto the tundra. What's taking Phoebe so long? Could she have hurt herself? Stumbled while crossing the log, twisted an ankle? Maybe it's a good thing after all that he's here. I certainly couldn't carry her by myself.

I'm shivering in the draft from the open door. "Oh, come in for a minute, then, if you want to." I move away from the door, onto the bed, leaving the packing box for him to sit on. As he walks into the room, I notice that he has a slight limp. He remains standing, his hands in his pockets. I get that feeling about him again—a sense of fear. Who is this man, after all? All of him seems—damaged. That's the word. His eyes look damaged, and his face.

"You don't look like an Alaskan, Captain Taylor. Have you lived up here long?"

"Just a year. I flew choppers in Vietnam. Then Cambodia. Best training there is, flying around in a jungle war."

Training for what, I wonder. I smile the barest smile of politeness at Captain Taylor. I listen as the wind changes direction again. I listen for Phoebe's footsteps on the gravel.

"There's a lot of work up here for pilots," he says, gazing around the room, over the walls and the floor, pausing for a moment at the closed back-room door. "Hell, people fly up here the way people in the lower forty-eight drive cars."

I'm not sure what to ask now. I would like to win his sympathy enough to get him gently, finally out the door—no fuss, no muss. I speak quietly. "It must have been awfully hard on you, Captain—What's your first name?"

He fidgets and looks down at his feet. "Taylor's my first name. It's just a nickname, Captain Taylor. I didn't ever make captain."

"I'm sure you did a good job, though, Taylor. It must have been difficult. It's probably still difficult, flying through all this weather up here."

"Oh, the mining gigs are a piece of cake. You should see the way they feed us up there in the DeLongs—steak and fresh milk every day; a different movie every night."

I think briefly about the empty muffin plate—and the injustice of it, in light of this new information. But of course I don't say anything.

I stretch as well as I can with the sleeping bag over me; and smile at Taylor, yawning. "You know, I've had such a nice time talking with you, but I'm so tired. You'll excuse me, won't you, if I ask you to leave now so I can get some rest?"

"I'll stay and watch you," says Taylor. "I'll guard the door. Where's that gun of yours?"

I am careful not to look toward the back room. I look into Taylor's eyes instead, into his goaty, expressionless eyes. He is crazy. He's not telling me everything. We've both been playing a game of charades.

Blue, the ferocious killer dog, has fallen fast asleep at the foot of Phoebe's bed. I get up again. "I want you to leave now," I say in the same quiet voice. I make just the slightest move toward the back of the room, still facing Taylor.

He comes up close to me, smiling. I smell the stink of his breath. He grabs my forearms with his impossibly small hands, like the hands of a child. They're strong, though. He's hurting me.

"Let go of me, you little prick!" I shout at him at the same moment that Phoebe comes stomping in through the door from outside.

I kick him between the legs and he doubles over, moaning. "Cunt!" he shouts at me; then he looks at Phoebe. "Lesbo cunts!" Blinking his eyes, he reels around first at me and then at Phoebe; he's roaring like an animal.

Phoebe swings at his jaw with her balled fist, a hard swing with the weight of her body behind it. His eyes as startled as those of a child who has been treated unfairly, Taylor stumbles backwards against the wall, under the oosik. He touches his face with his hands. They're covered with blood. He looks around wildly, he reaches up. Blue is barking now as I run into the back room for the gun. "Get back, Phoebe!" I shout behind me.

Another sound follows me, a sound that seems to exist by itself in a silent world, apart from the sound of the dog barking, the storm raging, the friction of bodies struggling, of clothing, and curses, and heavy breathing. It's a dull, soft sound of flesh and bone. It's a sound that above all the others makes my heart turn cold, a frozen lump in my chest.

I hear myself shout in a voice that comes out of a time before language, a time of primitive men and beasts and weapons. Phoebe is completely out of the way as I aim—curled up on the floor beneath him, sheltering her head. I cross my sights on Captain Taylor. He looks at me, and his eyes have changed: they're the eyes of an animal that knows it is about to die. I never thought I would have to use the gun. I aim at the chest and fire, just the way Phoebe showed me. I fire again.

Taylor lies dead in a horrible bloody mess on the floor, slumped over Phoebe, covering her like a second skin where she lies, unmoving.

Seventeen

It takes me a long time before I can lower the gun. The blood has stopped pouring out of Taylor, out of his ears and his mouth; out of his chest. I finally put the gun down when Blue has gone over and begun snuffling at the blood, wrinkling up his nose. "Get away!" I shout at him. I reach out and touch Phoebe's arm, sticking out from beneath Taylor; her flesh is still warm. Then I grab his arm, his dead arm, and pull hard with both hands until I feel as though my arms are about to pull out of their sockets. At first I'm dragging both him and Phoebe across the floor; and then he comes loose. It's a dead body, nothing more; it feels nothing as I drag it toward the door. Taylor's blood, mixed with Phoebe's, spreads out in a fan shape on the wooden floor.

And then I look down into Phoebe's face, touching her hair, the blood congealing above her temple. How can this have happened? We were supposed to come back from our tundra walk to hot tea and muffins; to another chorus of "The House Carpenter." To a mess of rice and beans, and then a long, well-deserved sleep. Her eyes are closed; the skin around her left eye is all discolored—yellow, purple. I think I can hear her heart beating, faintly, beneath my hand: I feel a flutter in her wrist as if from hundreds of miles away. I get the pocket mirror from the back room and hold it beneath her nostrils; it mists over with the palest wash of gray. The glass clears and then fogs over again as Phoebe's lungs labor inside her, while the animal of Phoebe's body struggles to stay alive. And then I run to the kitchen, grab a new sponge, and carry the pot of hot water back to the sleeping shed. I clean the blood from Phoebe's face and hands. I put her arm around my neck and ease her gently into my sleeping bag, zipping it up around her. Carefully I lift and put a pillow of clean clothing under her head. It's when I see all the blood underneath that I start to cry. "My God, Phoebe," I weep leaning over her. "You've got to be all right!" I am holding Phoebe and rocking her, resting my head on her breast. I am crying like a child in a nightmare, wanting to wake up, wanting to find it isn't true. But Phoebe's arms and legs are growing rigid; she's changing into stone, so beautiful, like a statue. I touch Phoebe's cheek and her nose and her eyes where the blood is swelling beneath her pale, translucent skin. I leave her for a moment to get the bit of bear undercoat and the whale's tooth that Robbie gave me; I wrap Phoebe's stiffening fingers around them. I tie Bill's handkerchief around her head.

I don't know what to do. There's no radio, and no planes are flying. There's the helicopter. The helicopter! There'll be a radio inside.

I kiss Phoebe's forehead and run outside, out behind the kitchen, where the helicopter sits like a huge dead insect. I climb up into its high belly. My electronic communication skills don't range far beyond the telephone. It takes me ages just to locate the radio among the myriad buttons and gauges and dials on the helicopter's control panel. They nicknamed me Miss Fix-It at the office—I was always the one called when the photocopier broke down, when someone dropped a contact lens into their type-writer; when no one could figure out how to draft tables on the new word processors.

I flick the toggle switches systematically, on, off, listen-ing in between. And then I hear static—radio waves! I press the call button. "Mayday, Mayday!" I say into the microphone, because this is what I have heard people say in the movies. "Medical emergency at the Darwin camp, on the coast between Point Hope and Kivalina. Someone has suffered a severe head wound. For God's sake, if someone hears me, send a plane!"

The static is alone for a long time, crackling. And then a woman's voice answers, accented and quavering over the airwaves. "Camp Darwin, Camp Darwin," says the voice. "This is Point Hope. We've received your message. Hold on, lady. Help is on the way."

I walk back to the sleeping shed and I can smell it: thick and sticky, salty and foul—the smell of death, of blood. I won't leave Taylor in the same room with her. Grabbing him under the arms, his head lolling backwards, I drag him bumping down the steps, outside, bit by bit across the gravel, pausing every few feet to catch my breath in the rain. I didn't think I could do it alone, but I drag his body all the way to the other sleeping shed—the one that Phoebe shared with Mike. I drag him up the steps and over the threshhold, and I feel connected to him—this murdered bridegroom, this other Tay. I look down into his nightmare eyes, rolled back into his head like the eyes of the dead murres. I close his eyelids over the gaze that was as lifeless before as it is now. Did I put him out of his misery? Does one life matter—or two? Or three? Does he have a girlfriend waiting somewhere, waiting to see him again? A mother who remembered his eyes before they deadened up, hardened over? I look down at my hands, stiff and caked with blood. I think of the baby bird, its wings broken, its death looming above like a shadow. Somewhere, someone called Taylor's number. I pulled the trigger, but I never planned it that way; I never wanted it to happen. I look down at the dead helicopter pilot and whisper, "I'm sorry." I don't even know his last name.

I hunker down further into Phoebe's sleeping bag, where I've curled up next to her on the floor, my arm slung over her. The rain is still falling outside, the windows breathe in and out. I listen for the sound of a plane. Then I fall asleep, but I wake up when Blue is crying, asking to be let out. I walk him outside, we both pee; I give him some dog food in the kitchen. I drink a cup of water. When we walk past the blood again, Blue sniffs at it, tries to stay there, tasting it, trying to understand. I have to pull him away, tugging hard on his collar. The water's already cold, but I scrub the blood away, sweeping it outside with a broom, spreading it in a pale brown wash over the floor. Then I lie down next to Phoebe again. Blue curls up at my feet, knitting his eyebrows and sighing as he falls asleep. I am watchful, sleepless. Nothing moves but the windows, sucked in and out by the wind; or Blue, shifting in his sleep.

Then there's a long darkness, a brown tunnel. Facts are like leaves on a forest floor, decomposing. I hear myself think as I fall, "Thank God!" and then all is thick night with images that shimmer up like moths and brightly colored pieces of glass. I can see the china shop. Sunlight breaks up into rainbows in the cut crystal and dances on the walls and ceiling. Phoebe's uncle is there, an old man with a kind face and a white mustache. The light is golden, and there's a kind of music, but it seems to be part of the light, not like music at all, but more like the wind. And then all the crystal teardrops surrounding the candlesticks and the chandeliers begin to knock together like Tibetan bells, and there's another sound—the biggest motorcycle the town's ever seen. It arrives from nowhere, it's sent by God. It's come to take Phoebe away from home, away forever. The old man smiles, but there are tears in his eyes and on his cheeks. The sound of the motorcycle swallows everything.

I wake up, but the sound is still there. I look around, frightened. I go into the back room and stand up on the cot to look out the window.

There are three motorcycles out on the gravel, all bright red and chrome, each with three wheels blown up like tractor tires. I half-expect to see Mike because of my dream, but these are men such as I've only seen before in Kotzebue—Eskimos, with ancient Asiatic faces and tired eyes. They stand looking off into a middle distance and waiting.

I walk out as I am, my watch cap pulled down low, my face and hands stained with tears, blood, and rain; my body stinking. I hold my jacket close around me; I'm cold. I don't know what to say to the men. The oldest one nods. The youngest one, who is fat and a little jolly, asks if they can rest for a while. "Been riding all night," he says.

I lead them into the kitchen. We all look at the shotgun, then look away. I fill a pot with water and scrub my hands. Then I make coffee and pancakes. We eat together from paper plates, on folding aluminum chairs. When we're finished, the two younger men, without ceremony, fall asleep, one stretched out on the floor, the other slumping in his chair.

"My nephews," says the older man. He looks at me searchingly. He seems to consider carefully before he speaks again. "There's something here for us."

Beginning to understand, I nod at him. The man nods back, then just as suddenly as the others falls asleep.

I tiptoe out and walk quietly back to the sleeping shed and sit beside Phoebe, stroking her hair. It seems so strange that the hair is still so beautiful and alive (I avoid the side that's caked with blood), while Phoebe's face is white marble, her lips gray, all the blood gone from them. I fall asleep draped over the body that lies uncorrupting in the cold. Then Blue barks and wags his tail as the men walk in from outside, the youngest one faintly smiling even though he's wrapped his face in concern and solemnity, like a circus clown at a funeral trying to behave appropriately but longing to make everyone laugh.

We carry Phoebe together, two on each side of my sleeping bag. The old man wraps a blanket over her and ties her to the sled behind his motorcycle. I touch her hands through the blanket. Then I run into the kitchen and write down Phoebe's name and the Fairbanks address of James and Jacobs. Pressing the piece of paper into the old man's hands, I thank him. He nods and smiles kindly.

The men rev up their motors, then skid out over the tundra, northward toward Point Hope. I sob as I watch the sled bounce up and down over the rough earth. At the crest of the hill where I first saw the grizzly bear, so long ago, the motorcycles pause and the men stop to wave at me. I wave back, and stand for a long time in the drizzle, long after they have disappeared.

Dear Morgie,

I'm going to have a baby. Robbie doesn't know, and I'm not even sure I'll tell him. He left about a week ago to return to medical school. It wasn't a conscious move on my part. I don't know what I was thinking of, but I never even bothered using my "contraption," although I had it with me. I guess it was just time.

Everyone's gone now except me and Blue, and this baby growing inside me. The men all flew off, leaving me and Phoebe alone; we were expecting reinforcements for the work up here, but then a huge storm blew in, making it impossible for any planes to land. Then a helicopter landed, in the storm, and the pilot got drunk and bashed Phoebe's head in with a walrus penis bone. I know, I know—it just sounds too bizarre, but that's exactly what happened. I shot the pilot, but it was too late. I radioed for help, but instead of a plane, three angels of death on motorcycles took my Phoebe away with them.

I wouldn't dare tell any of this to anyone but you, Morgie—no one else would believe me. And here I am, pregnant, and completely alone except for Blue. Pregnant, and I don't even know whether there'll be some sort of inquest when I get back to civilization. I can't imagine there won't be. The strangest thing was that when I realized about the baby (or embryo or whatever it is at this point) I felt certain that it was Phoebe's, or even Phoebe. And ever since I found out, I've felt incredibly comforted (you can imagine what sort of state I was in to begin with).

It's been something like three days now since they took her away. My own feeling of reconciliation is one thing—but Phoebe's husband is due back any day now: and do you think he'll find any solace in my pregnancy or circus angels on motorbikes? I've even stolen his revenge. I know that you always considered me a sappy religionist (in my patchwork, pagan way)—but I'm sure that Phoebe's with God now, or the gods: and well she belongs with them. It's up to such mortal and weak-boned types as myself to stay behind and (literally) mop up the blood.

Dear old friend, how can I ever go back and pretend that everything's normal? I feel that a curtain's been pulled back and I've seen things that no one is meant to see. I'll never sit down at a typewriter again and type someone's god-awful report. When they first took Phoebe, I went sort of crazy—I kept shouting for her, shouting up into the sky, over the tundra, until I was too hoarse to shout any more, until I was coughing up blood. And then I looked at the calendar, and counted backwards, and figured it out. Oh, I know what you're thinking—just some sort of traumatic reaction. But I know it's happened. I even feel different—you know, nauseated. The way you're supposed to feel. I just touch my toothbrush to my tongue and I feel like I'm going to throw up.

And now it's just a matter of waiting—until the plane comes, until the baby stops looking like a tadpole and grows long fingers and gorgeous skin and hair, and slanted Modigliani eyes. I already feel huge and swollen and ripe. Envy me, Morgie—I am full of life.

—Tay

Eighteen

~~~~~~~~~~~~~~~~~~~

The wind sucks at the windows like a hungry mouth, the rain blows in great gusts against first one side of the kitchen then the other. Fog blows over the camp and I am swaddled in white darkness, a timelessness in which I feel short of breath and panicky. Have I imagined it all? Did I die, and is this what it is like to be dead, to have no tests of reality, no second voice to confirm what is and what isn't? The wind-up alarm clock on the scientific table has run down, stopped. In a panic, I wind it up again. But where am I to set the hands? And what does it matter?

The meaningless ticking is horrible. I feel like prying off the face, smashing the works to silence. Then I throw the clock out the window, onto the gravel. Suddenly it all seems very funny to me, like the punchline of a joke. The wind dies down and I can still hear the clock ticking in between the sound of the waves smashing up on the shore.

Blue starts howling, God only knows why. I stanch my ears with my hands until I hear another sound, and I realize that it's coming from me, from deep inside me, the sound of an old peasant woman moaning and keening, following a coffin. I hold my hand over my mouth.

Then Blue is silent, and we sit and look at each other. I mustn't let Blue think I've gone completely crazy. I walk as calmly as I can outside; I pick up the clock. Then I boil water for tea.

The weather is changing—still raining, but more lightly now. Groups of birds are clumped up, flying south. I am scanning the sea with binoculars when a jet of spray shoots into the air. I watch for it to happen again, itching to have someone to ask whether or not it's a whale. I've never seen a spouting whale before; it only happened once, and so quickly I'm afraid I've imagined it. But who's to say, really: to confirm or to deny—it's my decision, after all. I'm the only person in the world who saw it at that very moment, spouting, just like the whales that Melville described. It's my whale—my relationship with the whale.

Phoebe would have seen it, too—would have confirmed it; but Phoebe is dead. In my belly there's something that looks like a tiny fish. It floats inside me, its eyes closed. But if it opened its eyes, I would see that they look like Robbie's, a liquid dark brown with one slightly larger than the other, eyes from another climate, of camels and blood-red sunsets and prayers that curl in strange tongues over the landscape. Or perhaps the eyes are green and slightly long, and the skin is very pale, the skin that Rubens painted, ivory and pink, skin with a look of the bone beneath it, skin as white and gleaming as a walrus skull in the moonlight.

*   *   *

I'm sharing a rain puddle with Blue, having a bath, when I hear a plane overhead. Blue hears it, too. I dry off quickly, put on my clothes, and run back up to the kitchen, bursting through the door.

Mike and Strider are there, and Bill with another man I don't recognize, and two people who can only be Ned and Kate Rogers. They nod and smile at me; I think they've both said their names, shaken my hand. All I can think of right now is how I'm going to tell Mike.

Bill reaches out and clasps my shoulder, shaking it a little, ringing me like a bell. "How are you, Tay?" He looks worried.

Then the tears start running down my face. "Oh, my God!" I turn to Mike and take both of his hands. "Mike! Oh, Jesus, Mike, she's—" I can't say the word. I ball my hands into fists and squeeze until my fingernails are cutting into my flesh. I've got to tell him. "Phoebe—"

Mike holds me by the shoulders and shakes me gently. "She's all right," he says.

I look back at him. I lick my lips. "Who's all right?"

"Phoebe."

"But, Mike—you don't understand."

"But, Tay, I do understand. She's fine. She's in the hospital in Fairbanks. She's going to be fine."

"But she was dead!"

Mike shrugs his shoulders. "I guess you've never seen anyone in shock before. It was losing all that blood. She came to in Point Hope. They stitched up her head in Kotzebue."

I look at Strider; he nods yes.

Phoebe. I form the word silently, looking around me,

beginning to smile. I turn to Ned and Kate, clasping their hands. "Oh, I'm so glad to meet you, finally, after all this time!"

I have to tell them about the other thing. The thing in Mike and Phoebe's sleeping shed, waiting for Bill to come, waiting with infinite patience. But I guess they knew—the other man is another helicopter pilot from the camp in the DeLongs. He has trouble meeting my eyes; I can't tell if he's afraid or ashamed.

We all push the door in together, hushed and frightened. Taylor is just as I left him, his eyes closed, his body slumped against the wall. Kate Rogers makes a gagging sound and runs out into the fresh air.

His hands have relaxed in death. I can see now that they weren't really as small as they appeared to be—he had simply held them half-closed, all tensed up. Now they lie open on the cement, like white tulips that have opened. I remember how they squeezed my forearms, how they hurt me. I remember the sound of the oosik as it hit Phoebe's skull. Taylor's dead but Phoebe's alive. Her number wasn't called.

We wrap Taylor in two green plastic garbage bags. The chopper pilot doesn't say much, but I notice the beads of sweat trickling down his forehead. Mike's hands are shaking. In some horrible way, Taylor belongs to me, will belong to me forever. I know that I will continue to see him, those eyes: suddenly moist with panic and fear, with the knowledge of death.

I don't go out to the runway with the others when the pilot revs up the helicopter to carry Taylor away. I stay behind to scrub his blood off the sleeping shed floor. All the same, no one will sleep in there again this year. Later on, perhaps—Eskimo hunters who need a place to stop and rest; a lost pilot. It bothers me that there is nothing to mark his passing, no gravesite; just the faint wash of blood-stained water on the floor. And even this will wear away.

I don't look at Bill's plane when it rises into the sky. I look down at my hands.

Ned Rogers is a big-faced man with gold-rimmed glasses and large white teeth in a crooked, attractive smile; Kate, his wife, has the look of a librarian even in her field-clothes. They have about them a feeling of homeliness and comfort (Ned, wet-eyed, shows me a picture of their four-year-old son, off spending two weeks with Kate's mother). They're happy and unglamorous; they take the edge off the past week's drama. They've brought fresh supplies with them: cucumbers and tomatoes, eggs and chicken and zucchini and potatoes and bread. Everyone wants to cook with these new supplies, even Strider. We're feasting three times a day. I'm sleeping in the back room again; Mike and Strider are settled in the main part of the shed. Ned and Kate have chosen to sleep in the kitchen, where it's warm.

Strider, Ned, and Mike were all at the University of Alaska together; they know each other well, and have a clear picture of the work to be done. Although not a biologist herself, Kate is an experienced fieldhand and a close observer.

Our plan is to count all the birds before they swim out to sea. No one knows where the murres go during the wintertime; if they roost on the ice floes, or float on the water, half-hibernating through the terrible months of darkness and cold. It's one of those strange migrations that no one understands—on a particular day, the murres simply leave the cliffs and swim out to sea. When it's summer again, when the days grow light and warm, the colony returns. Just like that—out of nowhere.

The good weather is holding—crystal-clear days and flat seas; the air is almost warm. I go out once with Ned and Kate to make final measurements of the kittiwake chicks at Colony II. I go out once with Strider and Mike to collect murres. It seems strange, in a way, that Mike is here instead of at the hospital—but he says that Phoebe insisted. There was nothing he could do to speed her complete recovery. The doctors are keeping her there under observation. But all the tests so far have come out well—no permanent damage; only the scar on the side of her head.

The kittiwake chicks have grown feathers; many of them are even bigger than their parents. Already they're starting to fly south, leaving during the twilight of night-time; the colony is thinning out.

Strider and I will count the murres at Colonies IV and V. Out of consideration for my seasickness, he and Mike wanted to leave me on the beach at Colony II with food and the shotgun to measure diurnal variations as the birds come and go on their daily routine of feeding and caring for themselves. But I want to be there at the sheer cliffs of Colony IV when the murres jump. Phoebe told me about it—it's a sight that hardly anyone gets to see. I've decided already that I won't let myself get seasick—and, anyway, the sea is as calm as it's been since the beginning of summer, clear turquoise in places so that I can look down and see the shadowy murres flying underwater as they dive and glide in pursuit of fish. Up above, against the black-dark cliffs, the birds look like bright dust-motes caught in the light. The beach is littered with large rockfalls and the stiff, rock-dusted bodies of birds that were killed in the storm.

It's late evening; it must be eleven o'clock. The sunset doesn't touch the sunrise any more—there's a bridge of half-darkness between them, light enough to find our way over the silent black waters, no longer light enough to count with any accuracy. But we've finished—at least Strider and I have finished all our counts at Colonies IV and V. We sit silently in the boat, shivering, riding up and down on the swell. We are tiny in the great empty darkness of sea and sky, of rock and wind. We're waiting because Strider said that he thinks it will be tonight. It's August thirteenth. The colony seems to be going to sleep. I am breathing in rhythm to this rocking motion, this gentle cradle rocking of the sea. I want to remember this sense of connection, this sense that all the salt liquid of my body, this sea within me, is part of this larger ocean; and I am at home here, as much at home as the sleepy murres on the edge of the cliff. As deeply rooted as the cliffs themselves, rising up out of the water. And I will carry this sea with me wherever I go, just as I'm carrying the baby inside me. The baby will be born in a spill of salt water, washed up onto the shore—and I will scoop it up in my arms, my child: this thing I've made.

And then it happens. Suddenly the parent birds begin flying up into the twilit air, swooping down into the water, diving under and popping up again. Within five minutes, they are all on the water, gathered into tight clumps, floating up and down on the swell. They open their mouths and throw back their heads and begin calling the babies down. It's a different call from any I've heard all summer long, a chortling vibrato: a call of encouragement, that pleads and threatens, that insists, that says, "Now!"

The chicks don't know what to do. They don't have their flight feathers yet. They're alone for the first time. They stumble along the edge of the cliff, crying out for their parents. They hear their parents calling up to them, hundreds of feet below on the dark water.

And I feel it all over again, how difficult it was, how frightening, to leave Peg and Denny, the safety of their nest, the safety of being a child. And how difficult it has been to leave the safe misery of my job at the university, to stumble forward into the empty space of my future. I wrap my hands round my belly: I'm carrying the next generation now. Peg and Denny will step down, fade into soft focus. They're really much older than I've allowed myself to realize—I've been seeing them as they looked years ago. They're in their seventies. They will see this child of mine; there will be a bridge between the sunset and sunrise, a bridge of soft gray light. And then I'll lose them. I'll have to be the adult, the elder; the artist.

It's twilight, when there's the least chance of the chicks being seen by predators. The chicks and the adults are speaking to each other through the darkness, the long chortle from the water, the high-pitched peeps of fear from the cliffs. And then Strider points, and I see something falling: one of the chicks has stumbled. It may hit an outcrop of rock and die, or a falcon may swoop down and grab it midair. Like a skydiver, at the last possible moment, the chick shoots out its leathery wings and glides down, hitting the black water and popping up again near our boat, its black beady eyes all startled, the adults swarming around it, full of congratulations, telling the other chicks that they should jump, too.

And then they all start dropping off the cliff, first one at a time, like rain just starting; then whole groups of them, and it looks like the cliff's falling apart, crumbling into the water, but it's just the chicks tearing themselves away and falling, full of animal faith, every cell bending toward that cry down below. And they know how to swim; they just know, even though they've never been in the water before. A few adults cluster around each chick that makes it and they shepherd it out to sea, calling and chortling at each other in the twilight.

And then they're gone, leaving a gaping hole in the air. The cliff's empty. Strider and I don't say a thing. We linger for a moment in the silence. The only thing we can hear is the lapping of the waves. There's nothing to keep winter from coming now. The summer's over.

Suddenly I feel cold. Strider starts the motor, and we head back to camp.

The census is completed. Our work's all done here. We board up all the sheds except the kitchen. All five of us sleep in the kitchen, our cots scattered over the room among the crates of gear all packed up and waiting for Bill's arrival. Then the weather changes. A storm blows in from the west.

One of the windows tears again overnight, but instead of putting on new plastic, Mike boards it up. Strider works at getting all the sample bottles correctly labeled, working by candlelight with the rapidograph. Ned sits at the scientific table applying Sno-Seal to his hiking boots. We haven't fixed a hot meal today. We're all hoping that Bill will somehow find a way to land. Maggots have appeared in our drinking water, probably from one of the walrus skulls. Kate says that the only sure way to make Bill land is to start something long and messy—she sifts the maggots out of the water and puts up a pot of beans.

There's no plane, though, and we eat the beans without much pleasure. We're all getting ready to go to bed when Mike, standing by the scientific table, suddenly starts cursing.

"I can't find my toothbrush."

Ned smiles sweetly. "Your toothbrush, Mike?"

"Yes, my toothbrush. It's a red one. I left it on the scientific table this morning."

Ned looks down at his boots. "You say it was a red one?"

"Yes, a red one. Have you seen it?"

"Well, I did see a red toothbrush on the scientific table. I was led to understand that what's on the scientific table is stuff for scientific purposes."

"Yeah, well I have scientific teeth," says Mike. "Did you use my toothbrush or something?"

"Well, yes, Mike, I did use it, I guess—at least I used a red toothbrush that was lying on the scientific table near the Sno-Seal. I used it to clean my boots." Ned retrieves the toothbrush from another spot on the table and hands it to Mike.

"You used my toothbrush to clean your boots?"

The corners of my mouth are twitching. I can hardly stand it. I don't dare meet Strider's eyes.

Ned is still smiling amiably. "Well, there it is, Mike—it's

not lost or anything." He plucks the brush out of Mike's fingers and begins to wipe the bristles vigorously against his jeans. "I could maybe boil it." He hands it back to Mike, who slumps down on the edge of his cot, looking as if he's about to cry.

"I just can't believe it," he says to no one in particular. Then, to Ned and to Kate as well, "It's not like I could go out to the drugstore and buy another one, you know!"

Ned doesn't seem to see either the humor or the pathos of the situation. "Look, Mike," he says. "You can use my toothbrush until we get to Kotzebue. Kate and I can share hers."

Mike looks up at him, his eyes dark with tears. "I don't want to touch anything that's touched your slimy teeth," he quavers. Then, to no one, "He used it to clean his boots."

I come over and sit down beside Mike, putting my arms around him. I know that he's thinking of Phoebe, not the toothbrush—I think it's hit him suddenly that she almost died. I start thinking about Taylor, slumped over, wrapped in garbage bags; how it might just as easily have been Phoebe or even me. How I've killed a man.

Mike cries just a little at first, and with terrible awkwardness, like someone who has completely forgotten how. The sounds he makes are ugly and strangled; his eyes grow bloodshot until he looks drunk. But then, especially when I start weeping quietly above him, his tears flow more naturally, and he clings to me like the last timber of a shipwreck in a storm.

We're all stuck in the one room together. Out of the corner of my eye, I can see Ned and Kate turning away as best they can. Strider gets into his sleeping bag and pretends to sleep, but I can see his shoulders shaking up and down. The whole room seems to be shaking in an orgy of laughter and sorrow. I don't know myself whether I'm laughing or crying. Mike speaks to me as if speaking through the grille of a confessional. "I wasn't there to protect her. It never would have happened if I hadn't gone away."

I hold him away from me and smooth back his hair, remembering (it seems so strange to me) that we were lovers. "Phoebe doesn't need you to protect her, Mike. Phoebe doesn't *need* protecting."

Mike looks down at his knees. "She isn't as tough as she pretends to be."

I wipe my nose on Mike's sleeve. "I keep forgetting that you've known her longer than I have." We're still whispering. "Mike—" I pause and look into his eyes again. "I'm pregnant with Robbie's baby."

Mike's face flickers for an instant with a smile. "Son of a bitch!" he says in a normal tone of voice. I put my forefinger to my lips and hush him. "Does he know?" he asks me.

"Of course not! I only realized myself a week and a half ago."

"Are you going to tell him?"

"Maybe. Later, I guess, when it's too late for him to do anything about it."

Mike's serious again. "You're going to have—an abortion?"

"Jesus, no! I'm going to have the baby." I smile at Mike, then add, "I want it more than anything right now."

He sighs. "I envy you."

"You can be godfather."

"Oh, Strider will want to do that."

In the half-darkness, Strider raises his bulk up on one elbow. "Did I hear my name used in vain?"

"That's probably not all you heard, big ears," says Mike.

"Well, what do you expect?" he whispers. "If you don't want people to listen, don't have such interesting conversations!" Then he looks at me, smiling a little stupidly. "Son of a bitch!" he adds.

"I might object to that phrase." There's a pause. "Are you going to tell Robbie, Strider?"

"Not if you don't want me to. But I think you should. Mosher's no dummy. He knows where babies come from."

Kate's voice comes across to us in a thin whisper. "Are you having any morning sickness, Tay?"

"What the hell are we whispering for?" says Strider. "The whole world knows."

"Let's have a drink to celebrate," says Ned from the shadows. He strikes a match and lights a candle.

"Who has any booze? You been holding out on us, Rogers?"

Ned rummages in his pack. "I was just saving it for a special occasion." He finds and displays a bottle of apricot brandy. Strider pads out of his bag and fires up the heater. I slip a huge chocolate bar out from under one of the boxes and break it into five parts. Blue wakes up and walks from cot to cot nudging our knees and sniffing our hands.

"To Tay and Robbie's baby!" toasts Ned, breaking the seal and taking a pull from the bottle. He wipes off the neck with the hem of his shirt and hands it to Kate.

"Here's to you, Tay! You'll make a wonderful mother." Leaning out from her cot, she gives the bottle to Strider.

"To my godson!" he says, drinking and handing the bottle to Mike.

Mike looks across at the candle. He looks so handsome for a moment in the firelight, like a young girl's fantasy of what a handsome man looks like. And then the candle wavers, wrinkling and distorting his face into a vision of the future—of a man no longer boyish and winsome, who will have to lean more on his wits and his soul. "To Phoebe," he says. He drinks and turns to me. "Maybe if it's a girl you'll name her Phoebe."

I take the bottle from him. I don't drink—I'm ready to give up all such vices for the next eight months—but only toast in the air. "To Phoebe!"

Nineteen

I'm still sleeping when Bill walks in—I didn't even hear the plane land. I prop myself up on one elbow and look around. We simply fell asleep as we were last night, inside and outside sleeping bags. The empty brandy bottle is on the floor. Blue is butting his head up against Bill's legs.

"Holy Mother of God! This looks like the Fairbanks mission." Bill nudges the hulking shape of Strider in his sleeping bag. "Wake up, slug-a-bed! We've got to have the plane loaded up in two hours or else we're all going to be here till next spring, and it looks like you've already drunk all the Christmas cheer."

We all peel out of our sleeping bags, stretching, scratching, and groaning. When we've pulled our clothes on, Bill supervises our packing—and suddenly it's like leaving childhood behind. Everything in the camp draws my focus: every knothole in every weathered board, every rusty coil from the bedsprings; the dark, mysterious shitter and the panorama from the shitter outside with the huge horrifying mound of our excrement behind the makeshift platform and the wild arctic sweep all around—the wilderness that dwarfs even the monstrousness of our shit; that makes us small, that encompasses and includes us.

We load on the crates of salvaged bones, the tents and cookstoves, the outboard motors, the rubber boats, the hip boots, the life preservers, the extension ladders, the hard-hats, the baby moon; we load on our packs stuffed with imperfectly washed longjohns and stiff-legged jeans, bundles of driftwood and lovely pebbles, treasures washed up on shore, battered field-notebooks. We carefully pack our binoculars and shotguns and shells.

The kitchen is denuded, in twilight, the food lockers empty and gaping, the rough floor littered with tiny bits of our lives: fingernail clippings and hair mixed with feathers, sand, and bits of food—and something more intimate, the exhalations of our bodies, breathed in by the walls and mingled there with the breath of Eskimo hunters and army engineers, and the breath of Strider when he was ten years younger, and Phoebe's voice singing "The House Carpenter" and dissolving into laughter. It feels like we're stepping out of an old familiar body into an unknown infinity of space.

I sit in the co-pilot's seat next to Bill and watch the land fall away as we rise into the air and the whole camp falls into perspective. It's in the middle of nowhere, after all—at the northern edge of the world, across from the wasteland of Siberia; a tiny blot on the land. We're swallowed up by clouds, sightless, until the sky spits us out again onto the runway at Kotzebue.

Dear Morgie,

Passing through Kotzebue the first time, I saw a small outpost of exotic Eskimos making a rather pitiful go at being a commercial

Barbara Quick

town that catered to tourists and exploited its own quaintness: a couple of hotels and restaurants, several bars, a network of badly damaged roads leading nowhere. And now we're back, in transit to Fairbanks, and Kotzebue looks like the big city. Stepping out of Bill's plane, the first thing I noticed was the hardness of the tarmac under my feet. And then I heard the noise—a distant sound of trucks, the buzz of a chainsaw through the rain-soaked air.

Blue and I waited near the plane, finding shelter between some storage sheds, while the others went to get a truck and transfer our gear to the main terminal. They came back with the news that we'd already missed the flight out and wouldn't be able to leave until this afternoon.

We ate last night in the hotel restaurant, first taking hot showers and changing into our cleanest clothes. There's almost something obscene about all that hot water spurting out of a pipe in the wall and running down the drain beneath the floor. The toilet seemed strange, too—that sanitizing device that whisks everything away as if it never happened. I felt a sort of glum satisfaction when the toilet in our big communal room stopped up and refused to flush.

After dinner we walked down the street to the bar in the other hotel, and everything seemed impossibly garish, colorful, crowded, and smoky. A man at the bar stood up and smiled at me, and it took me a few seconds to figure out that he was offering me his seat. Then I caught a glimpse of a frail-looking woman in the wide crowded mirror among the glassware and swarthy faces. She was staring at me, a startled look in her eyes. She had strawberry-blond hair, freckles, and gray-green eyes.

I don't know who I expected to see. During the last eight weeks I've hardly looked at myself at all, and when I did I only saw a couple of square inches of myself at a time—one eye, my nose, my teeth, a patch of shoulder. Maybe I expected to see someone much bigger and stronger-looking: someone with raven-black hair and broad shoulders. It made me feel so strange, like someone freshly *born. I thought of the baby then—how it will be so strange for the baby being so completely new, seeing the world for the first time, all those bright lights and colors and shapes and smells.*

Walking back to the hotel in the middle of the dark road, we suddenly met a pair of headlights from a pick-up truck turning the corner, and I swear I felt fear before I remembered how to get out of the way. I looked into the lights with all the dumb terror of an animal.

I can see Phoebe as I walk through the door from the runway into the terminal. I remember how it was the first time I met her; how I walked behind her and Mike, filled with outrage, stinging with jealousy.

The bruises are almost gone. There's just the faintest touch of yellow under her eye, above her cheekbone. Her hair seems to cover the scar. It's funny the way things switch around: Phoebe and I are hugging. My eyes are closed, but then I open them. I catch a glimpse of Mike's face. The shoe's on the other foot now. I close my eyes again, feeling Phoebe, all alive and large and warm.

The intake officer at the county courthouse asks what my profession is. I am about to tell him that I work at the University of California; then I change my mind. I tell him to write "undecided." And then I tell him to cross that out and write "art student." He looks at me strangely but does what I tell him to do.

There aren't too many questions. The judge, dressed in a suit and sitting around a table with the other hearing officers, rules that I acted in self-defense. He tells me that I did the sensible thing under the circumstances. Then he tells me that I'm free to go.

I'm staying at Mike and Phoebe's cabin until I feel ready to leave. They built it themselves in the middle of a stand of paper birches where the first sound in the morning is the bell-like call of varied thrushes. I haven't grown tired yet of walking around the cabin, looking out the windows, looking at things that belong to Phoebe: her sewing machine, all set up and threaded with a spool of white cotton; some blown-up ads for sportswear and shampoo featuring Adelaide; an enlarged black-and-white photo of Phoebe's youngest sister warming up at a barre. Phoebe has books in every room. I like to think of her here in wintertime, curled up on the couch reading while Mike's teaching classes at the university; drinking nice cups of tea.

Strider visits us almost every night at dinnertime. He brings presents for the table. One night it was a bottle of French wine, then another time a slab of bear ribs wrapped in white butcher paper. Last time he brought us a silver salmon caught by an Indian friend. During the ice cream with chocolate sprinkles, he blurted out that if Mosher wouldn't have me, he would. I couldn't help laughing—everyone did; then I kissed Strider on his big broad cheek and he blushed. I was serious then. I put my hand on his arm and told him that it was nice to have so many options.

Phoebe whispers to me after dinner, while Mike and Strider are watching television. We put on our down jackets and our woolen hats, and walk out into the night, out the front door, into the yard. There's only a faint silvery light coming from the house, and the sound of birch leaves shimmering in the woods. The sky is black and we can see a thousand stars.

"Over there," says Phoebe, pointing.

And then I see them, swirling across the sky like liquid that is made out of light; shimmering like a curtain; pulsating with the muscular throb of horses, white, then pale blue, fuchsia, and greenish-gold. Northern Lights.

Phoebe and I stand side by side in the darkness making breath clouds, our heads thrown back. It's like a fireworks display just for us. At every change in the lights, we murmur *oohs* and *aahs* of appreciation. We watch, shivering, as the lights gallop across the sky, back and forth, finally settling into what looks like plain thin white clouds against the night sky, like a river of fog. Then they're gone. The sky is flat velvet again, pin-pricked with the fine hard points of stars.

Phoebe has promised to come down just before the baby's birth. She says that she doesn't know much about babies; she doesn't even like babies. But maybe if she sees me do it all right, she'll get up the courage herself. I think about this on the last leg of the flight to San Francisco. It makes me smile—the idea that I could teach Phoebe anything. The sound of the motor mixes with the lack of sleep to make something that sounds like angels singing, hard and high.

It's easy to pick out Peg and Denny among the swarm of faces at the end of the jet-way. Morgie is standing by a post further back in the waiting room holding a huge bouquet of sterling silver roses and baby's breath.

Getting out of the car at the end of the long winding driveway in Mill Valley, I look up at the black sky and pick out Orion, the Pleiades. Then I close my eyes and see birds against a twilit sky, miming a dance of constellations.

Afterword

It was a girl.